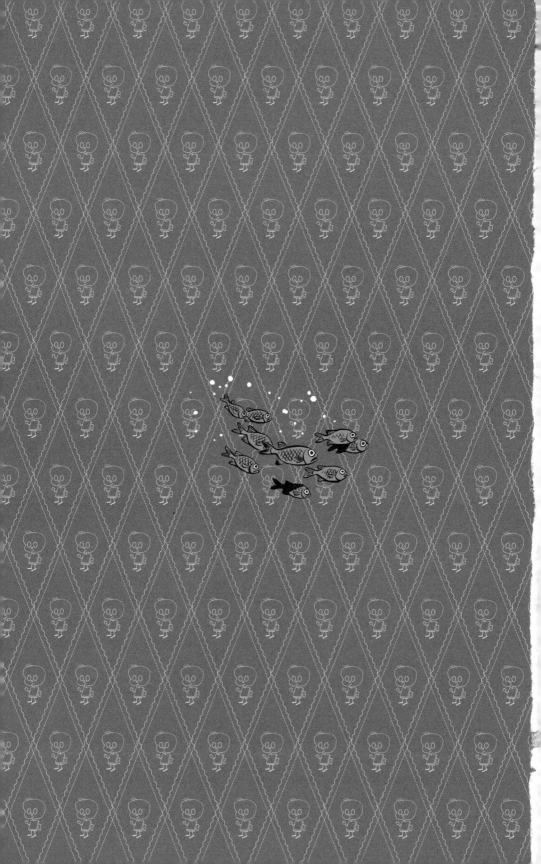

THE SHARK KING

R. KIKUO JOHNSON

A TOON BOOK BY

R. KIKUO JOHNSON

TOON BOOKS IS AN IMPRINT OF CANDLEWICK PRESS

For Danielle

A JUNIOR LIBRARY GUILD SELECTION

Editorial Director: F R A N Ç O I S E   M O U L Y

Book Design: F R A N Ç O I S E   M O U L Y   &   J O N A T H A N   B E N N E T T

R .   K I K U O   J O H N S O N ' S   artwork was drawn in ink and colored digitally

A TOON Book™ © 2012 R. Kikuo Johnson & RAW Junior, LLC, 27 Greene Street, New York, NY 10013. TOON Books® is an imprint of Candlewick Press, 99 Dover Street, Somerville, MA 02144. No part of this book may be used or reproduced in any manner whatsoever without written permission except in the case of brief quotations embodied in critical articles and reviews. TOON Books®, LITTLE LIT®, and TOON Into Reading™ are trademarks of RAW Junior, LLC. All rights reserved. Printed in Singapore by Tien Wah Press (Pte.) Ltd.

Library of Congress Cataloging-in-Publication Data:

Johnson, R. Kikuo.

The Shark King : a TOON book / by R. Kikuo Johnson.

   p. cm.

Summary: In graphic novel format, retells the Hawaiian story of Nanaue, born of human mother and shark father, who struggles to find his place in a village of humans.

ISBN 978-1-935179-16-0 (hardcover)

  1. Graphic novels. [1. Graphic novels. 2. Folklore–Hawaii.] I. Title.

PZ7.7.J642Sh 2012   741.5'973–dc23   2011026592

ISBN 13: 978-1-935179-16-0 ISBN 10: 1-935179-16-0

12 13 14 15 16 17 TWP 10 9 8 7 6 5 4 3 2 1

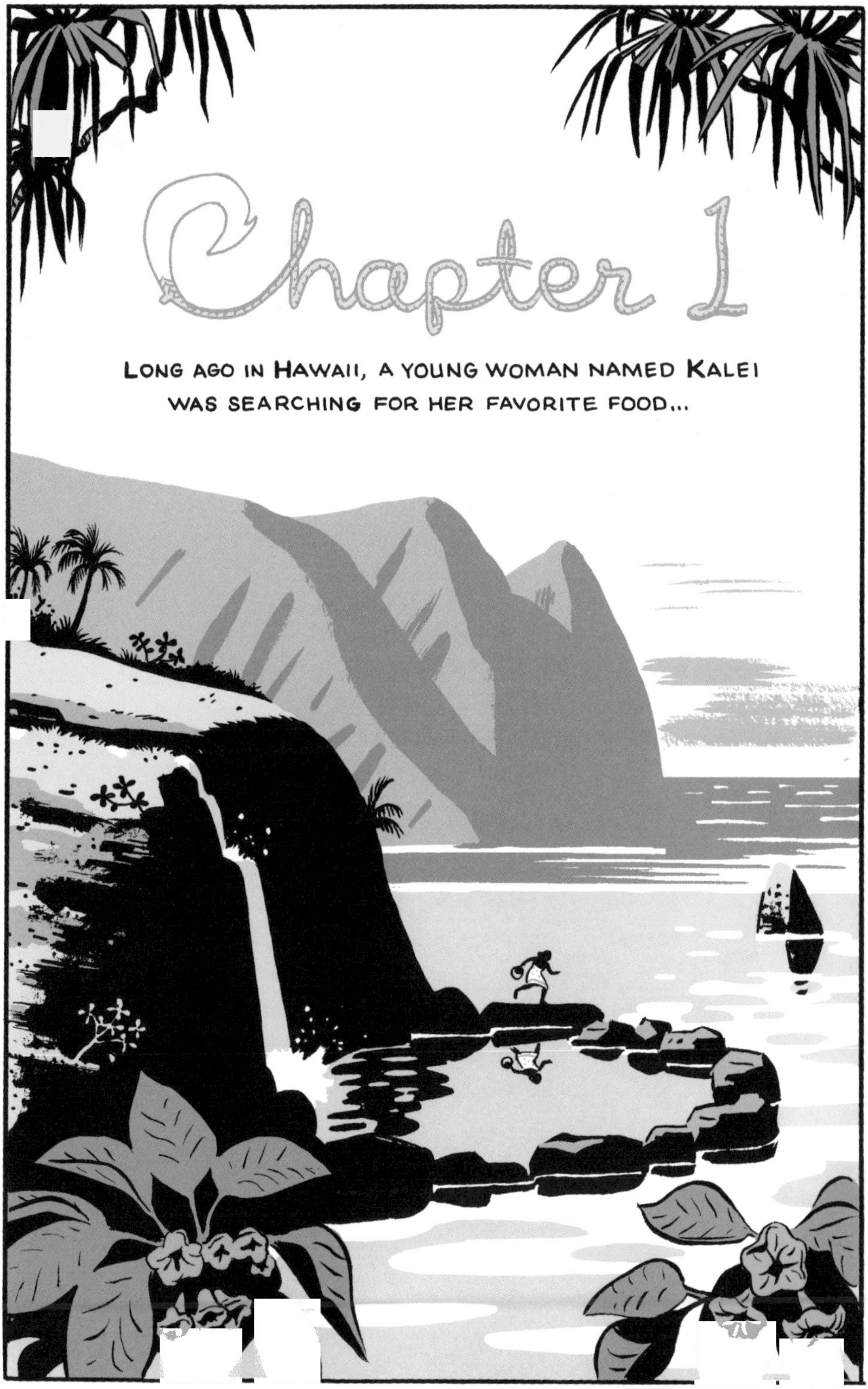
Chapter 1
LONG AGO IN HAWAII, A YOUNG WOMAN NAMED KALEI
WAS SEARCHING FOR HER FAVORITE FOOD...

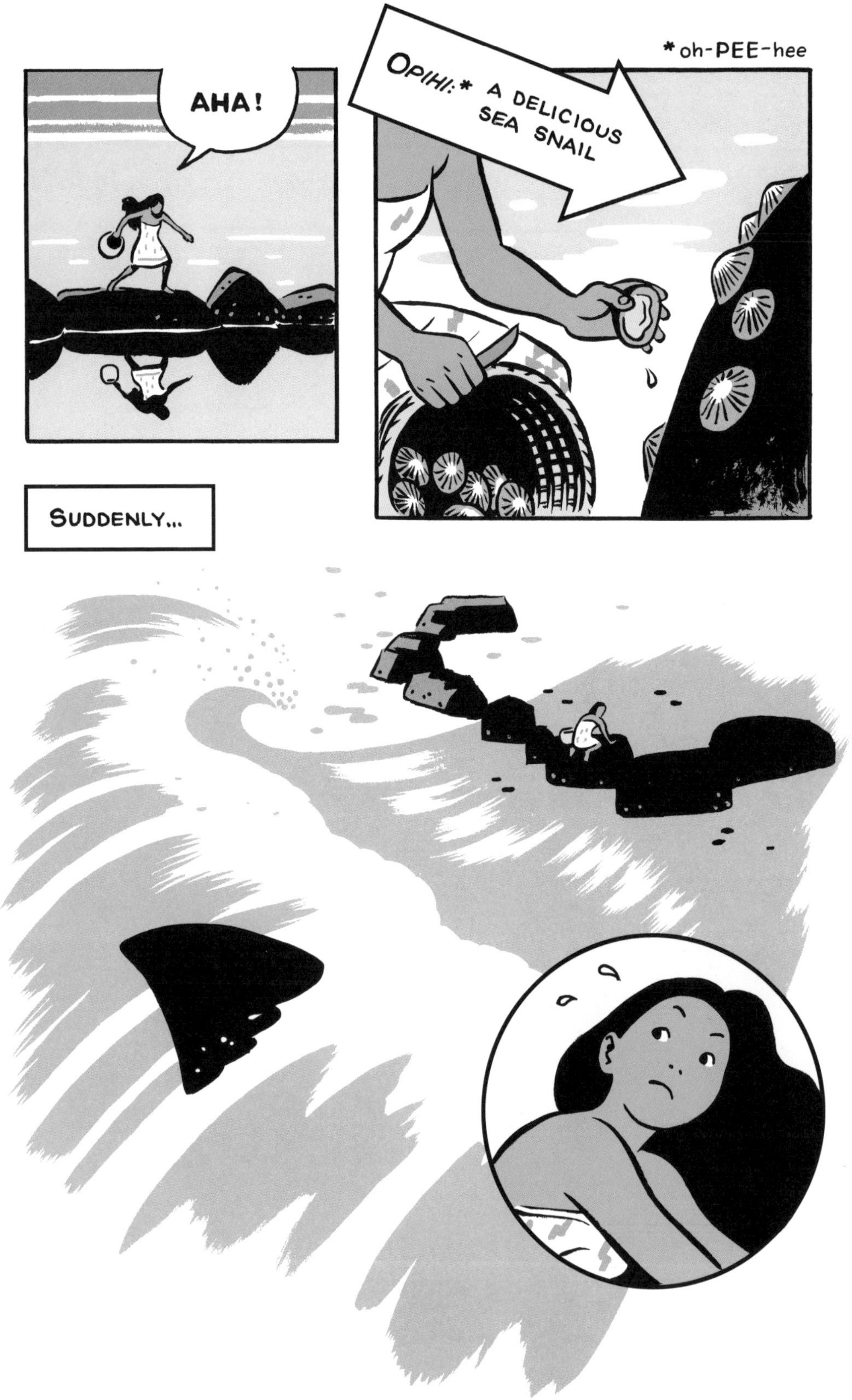
AHA!
OPIHI:* A DELICIOUS SEA SNAIL
*oh-PEE-hee
SUDDENLY...

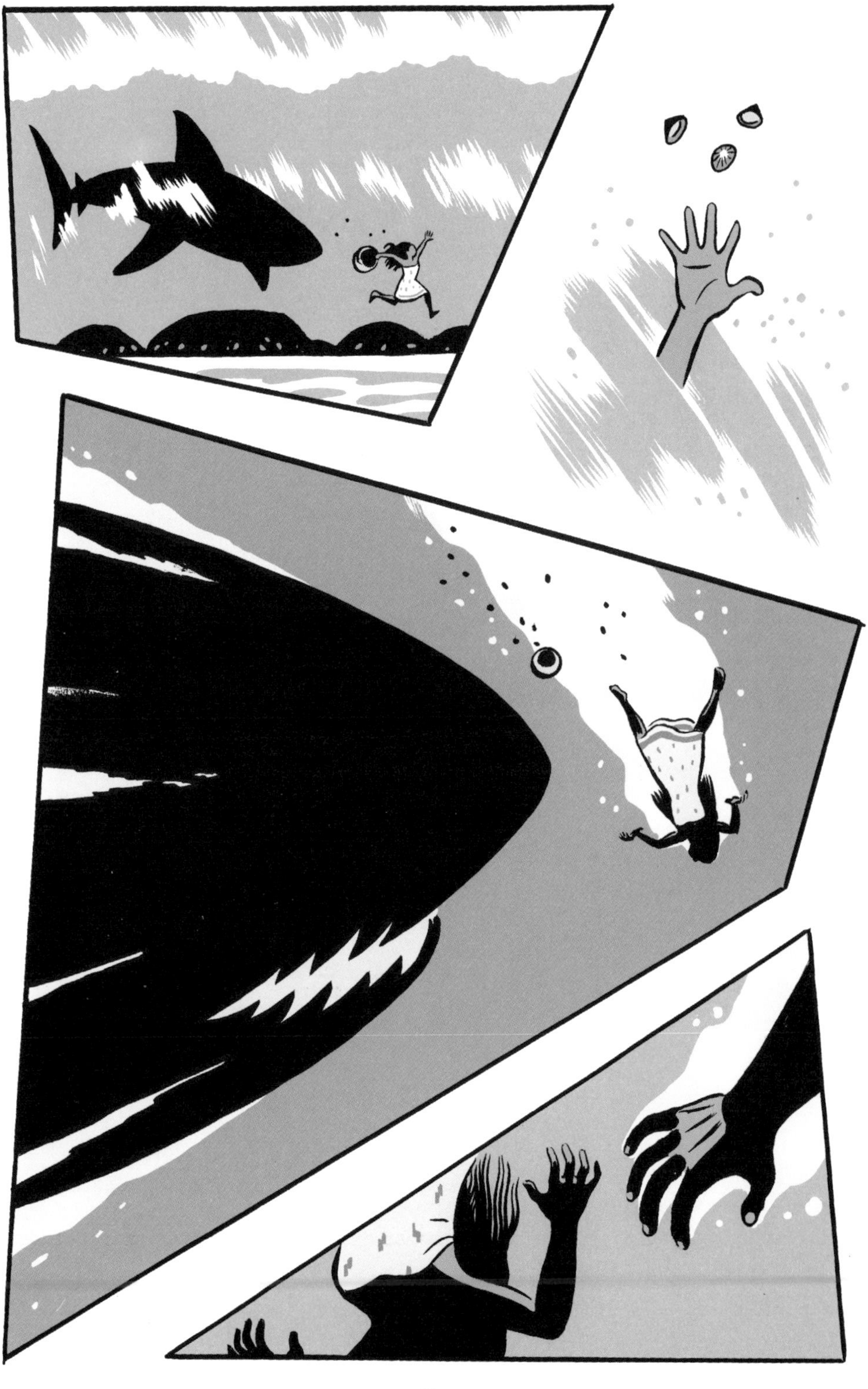

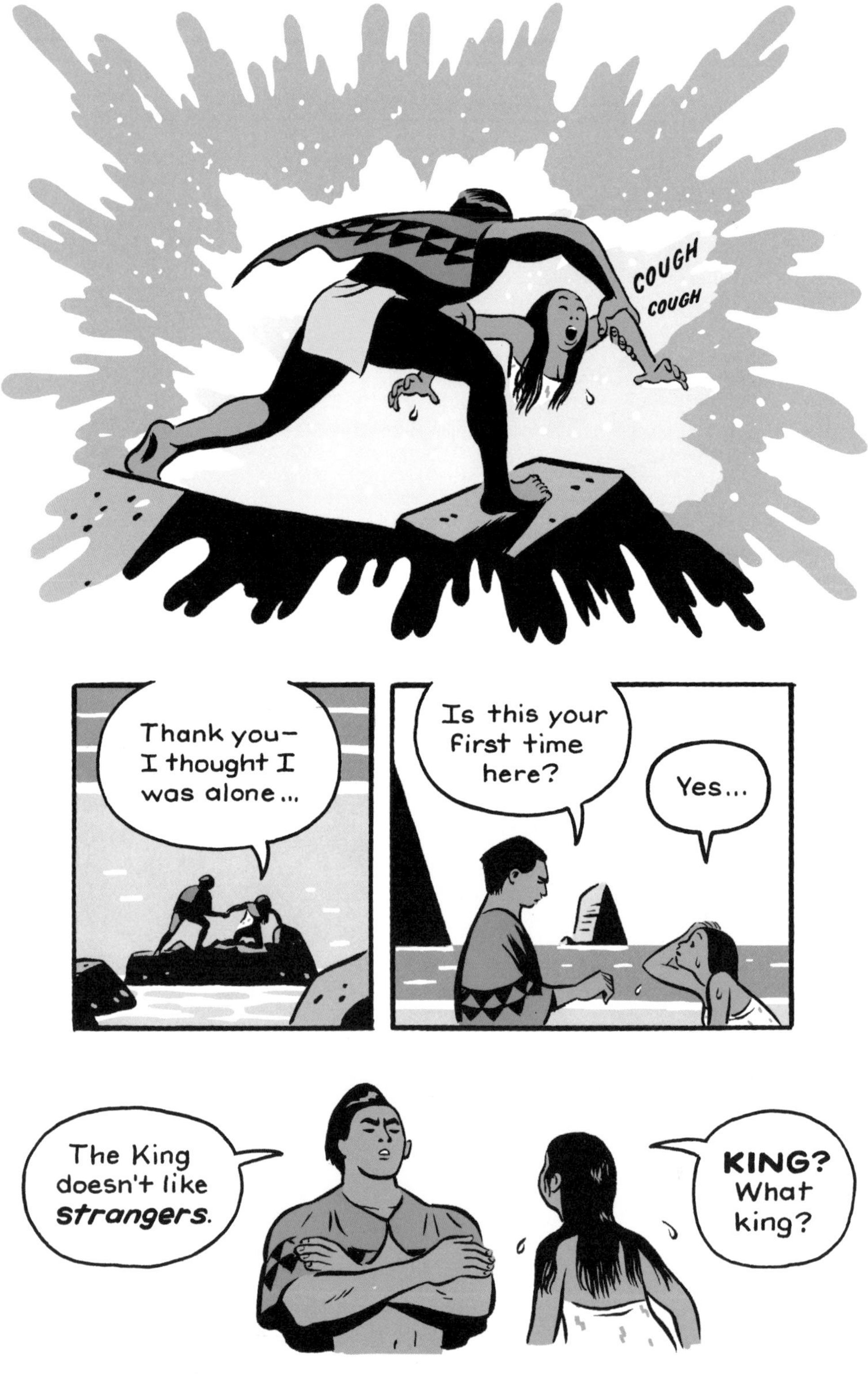
COUGH
COUGH
Thank you- I thought I was alone...
Is this your first time here?
Yes...
The King doesn't like **strangers**.
KING? What king?

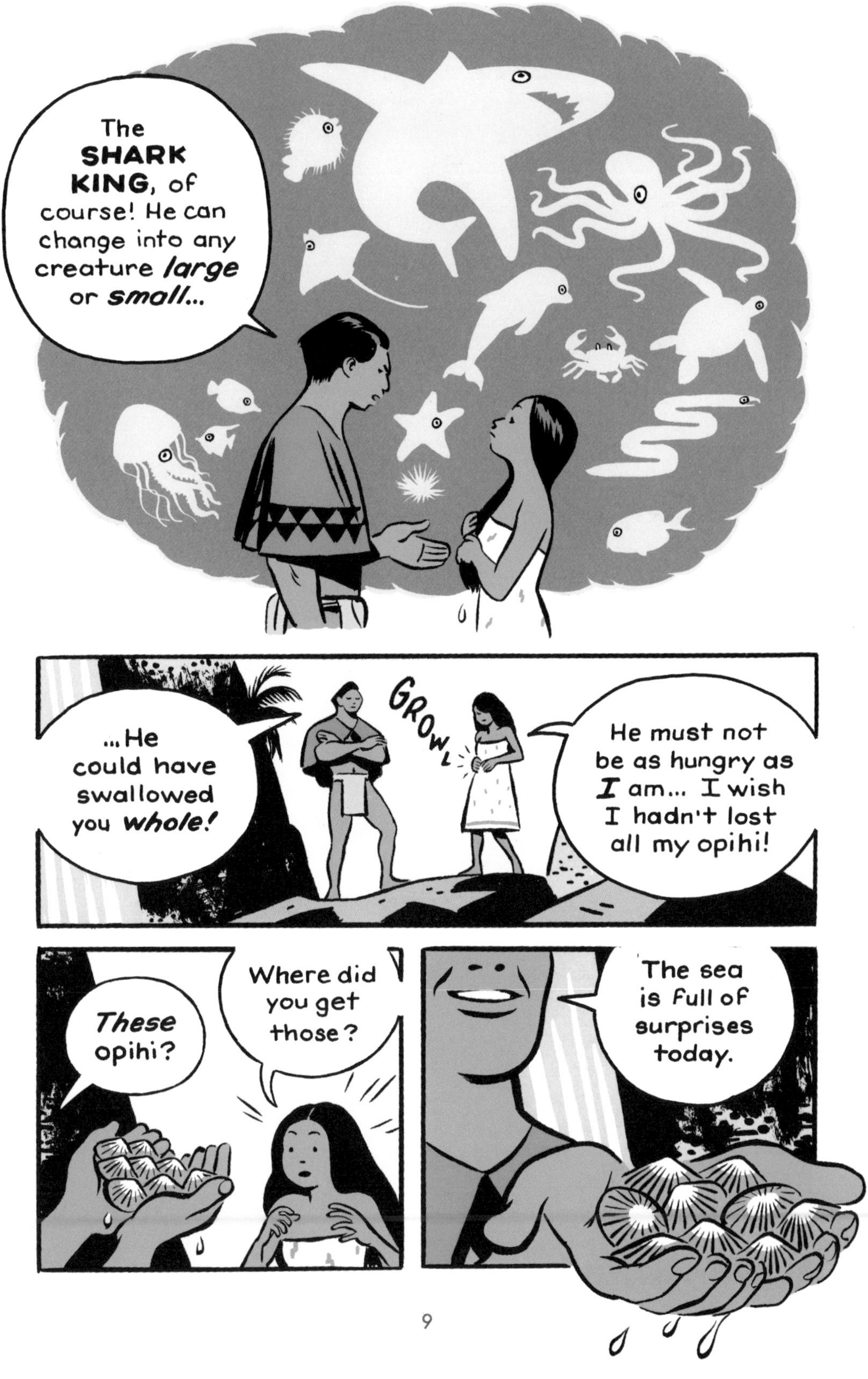
The SHARK KING, of course! He can change into any creature *large* or *small*...
...He could have swallowed you *whole!*
GROWL
He must not be as hungry as *I* am... I wish I hadn't lost all my opihi!
Where did you get those?
These opihi?
The sea is full of surprises today.

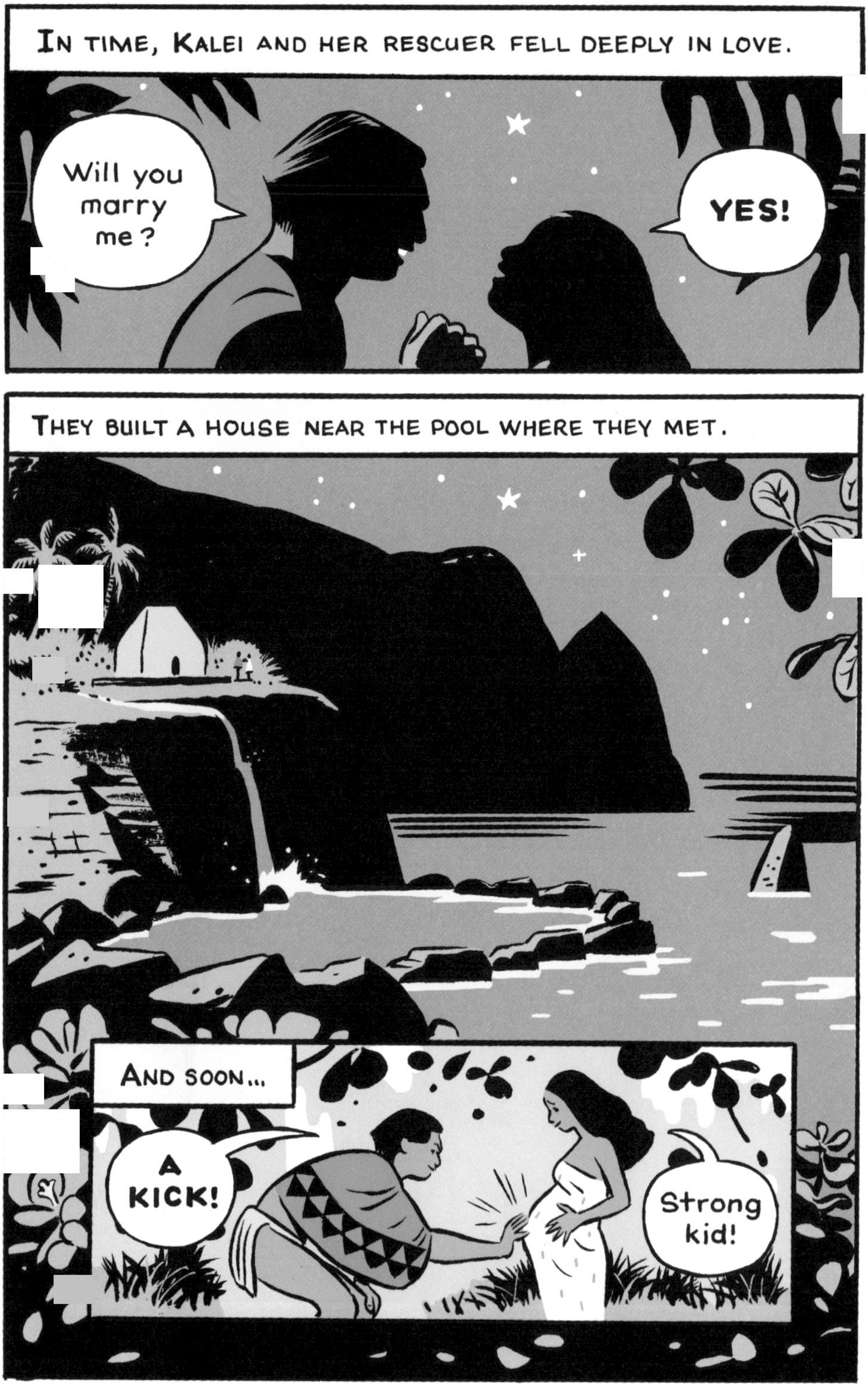
In time, Kalei and her rescuer fell deeply in love.
Will you marry me?
YES!
They built a house near the pool where they met.
And soon...
A KICK!
Strong kid!

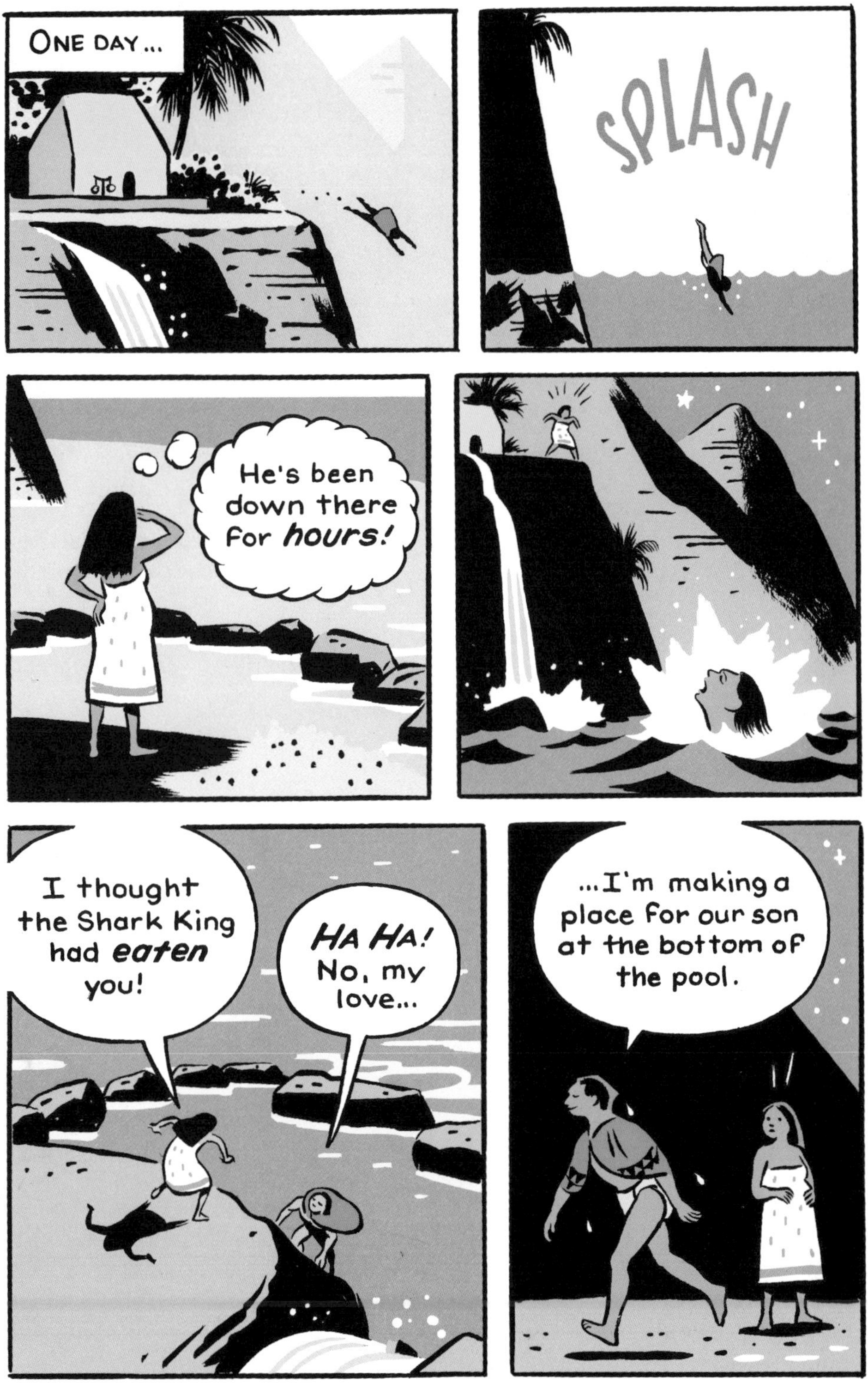
ONE DAY...
SPLASH
He's been down there for *hours!*
I thought the Shark King had *eaten* you!
HA HA! No, my love...
...I'm making a place for our son at the bottom of the pool.

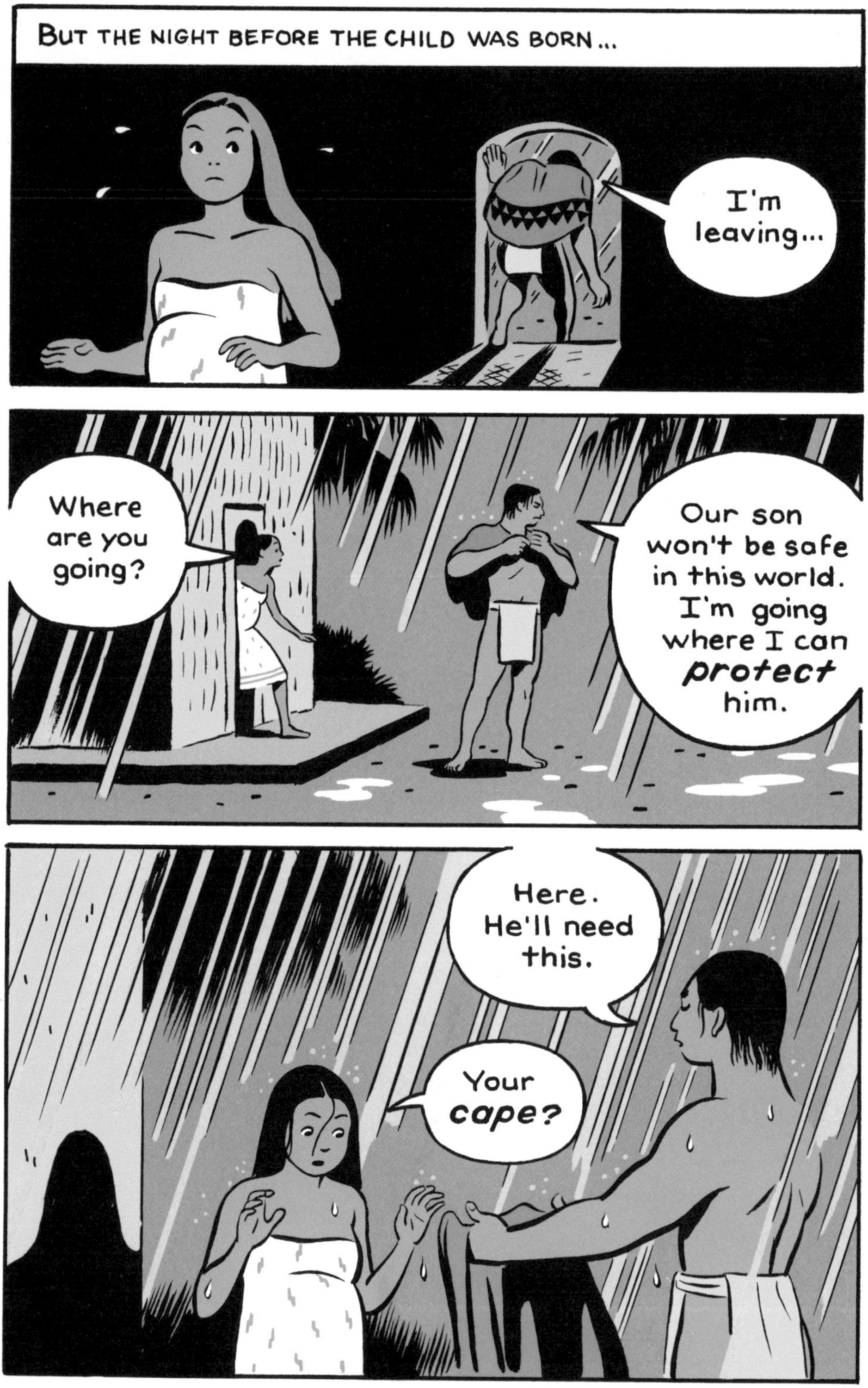
BUT THE NIGHT BEFORE THE CHILD WAS BORN...
I'm leaving...
Where are you going?
Our son won't be safe in this world. I'm going where I can *protect* him.
Here. He'll need this.
Your *cape?*

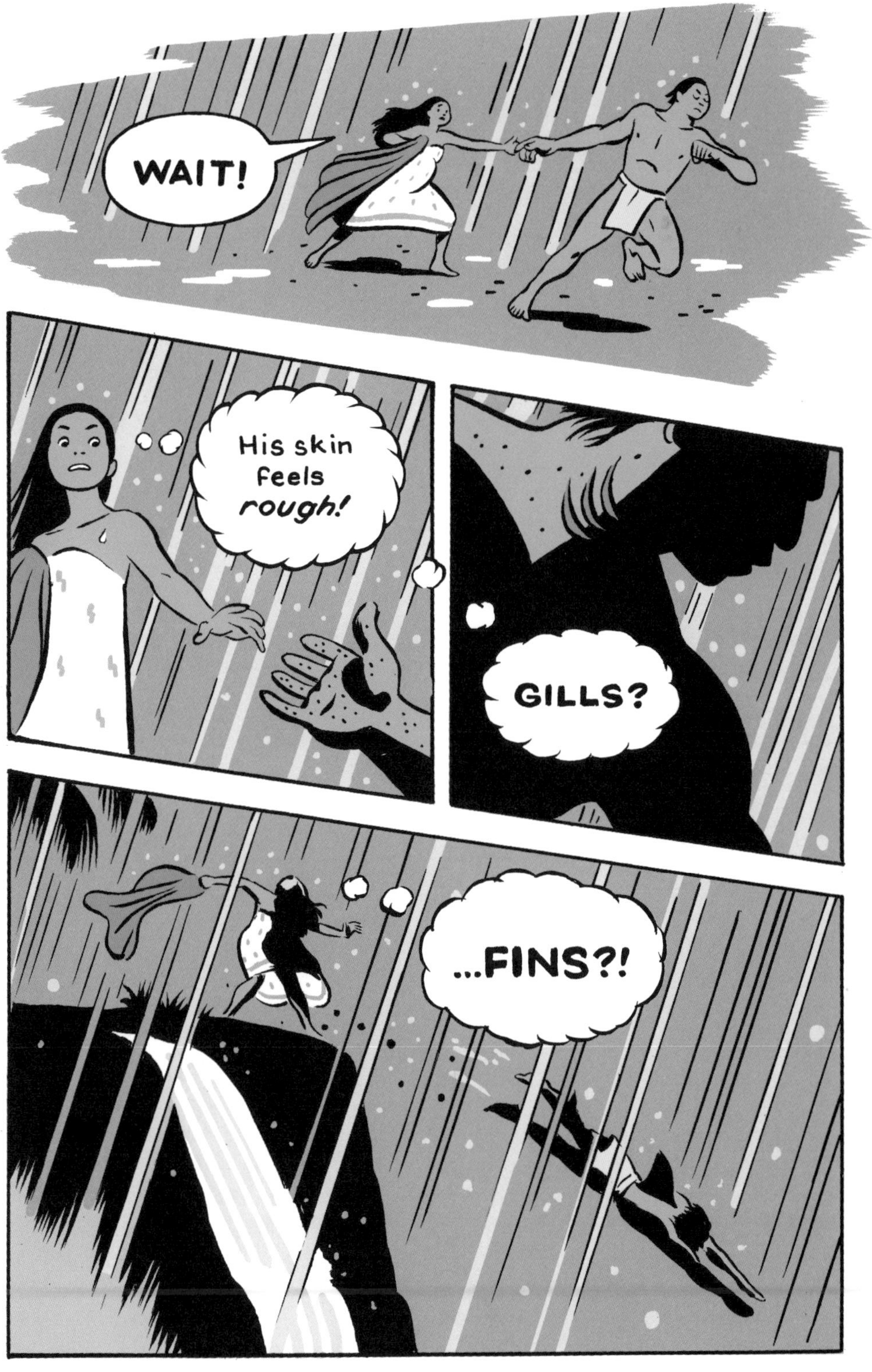
WAIT!
His skin feels *rough!*
GILLS?
...FINS?!

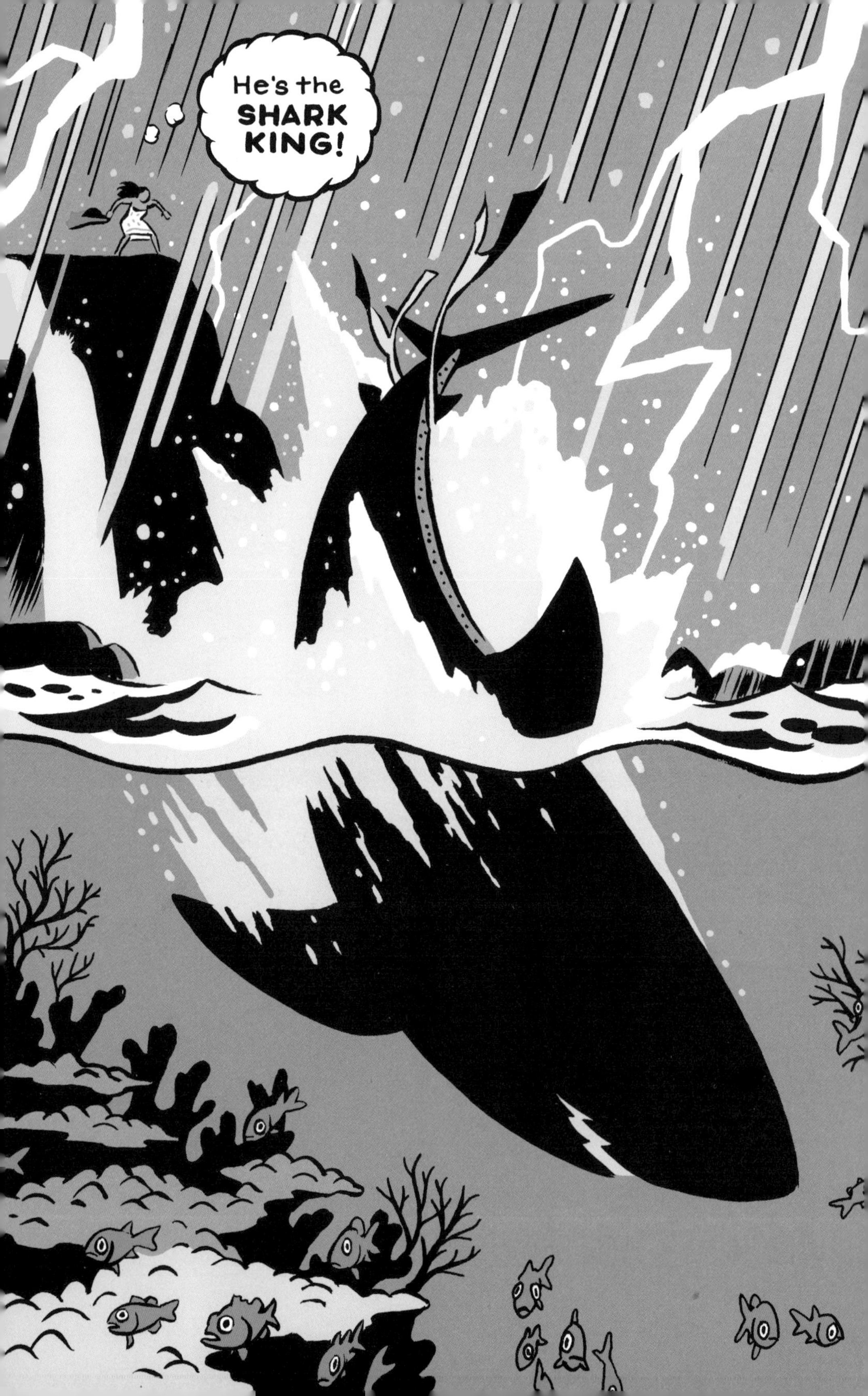
He's the SHARK KING!

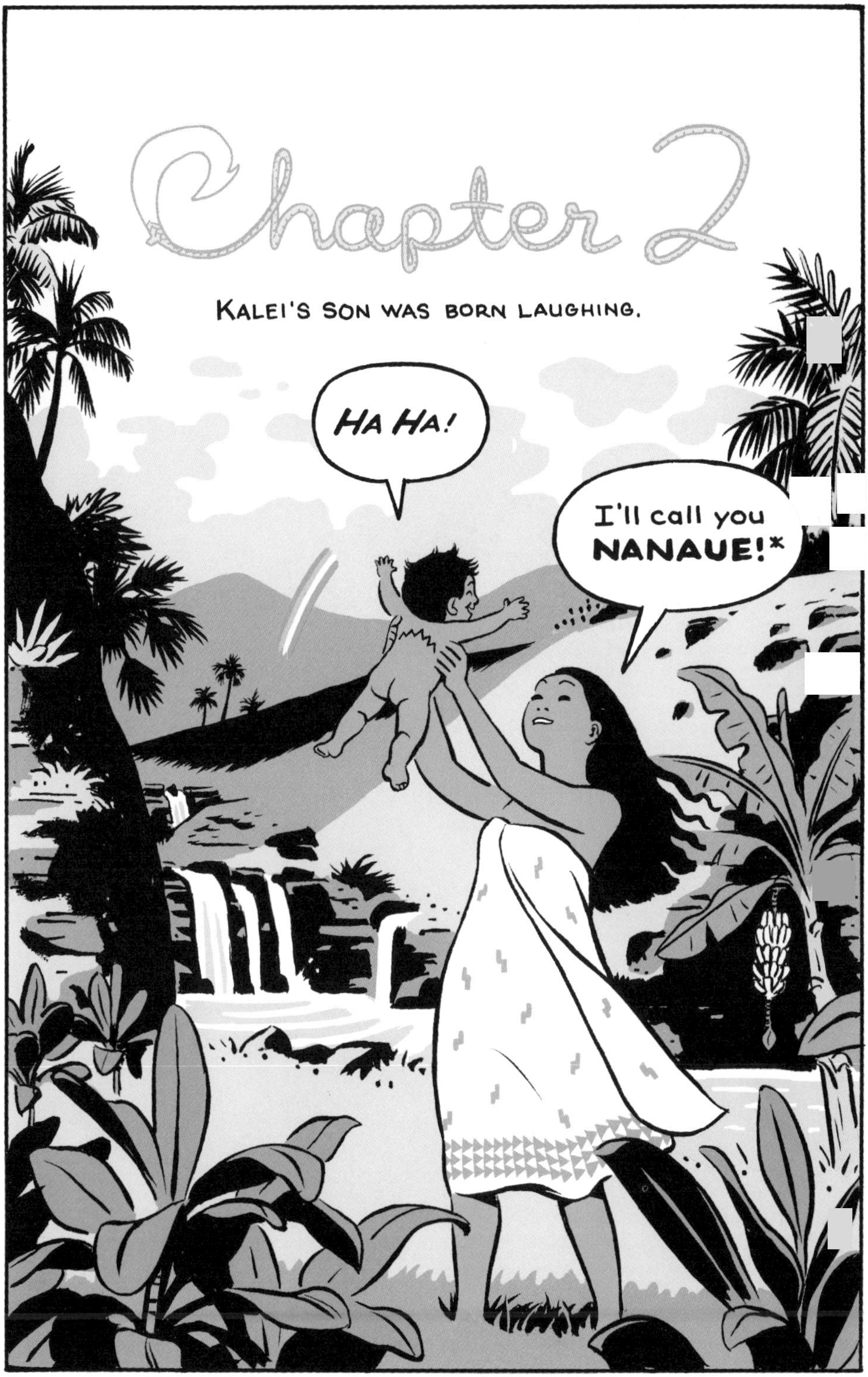
Chapter 2
KALEI'S SON WAS BORN LAUGHING.
HA HA!
I'll call you NANAUE!*

*nah-**NOW**-way

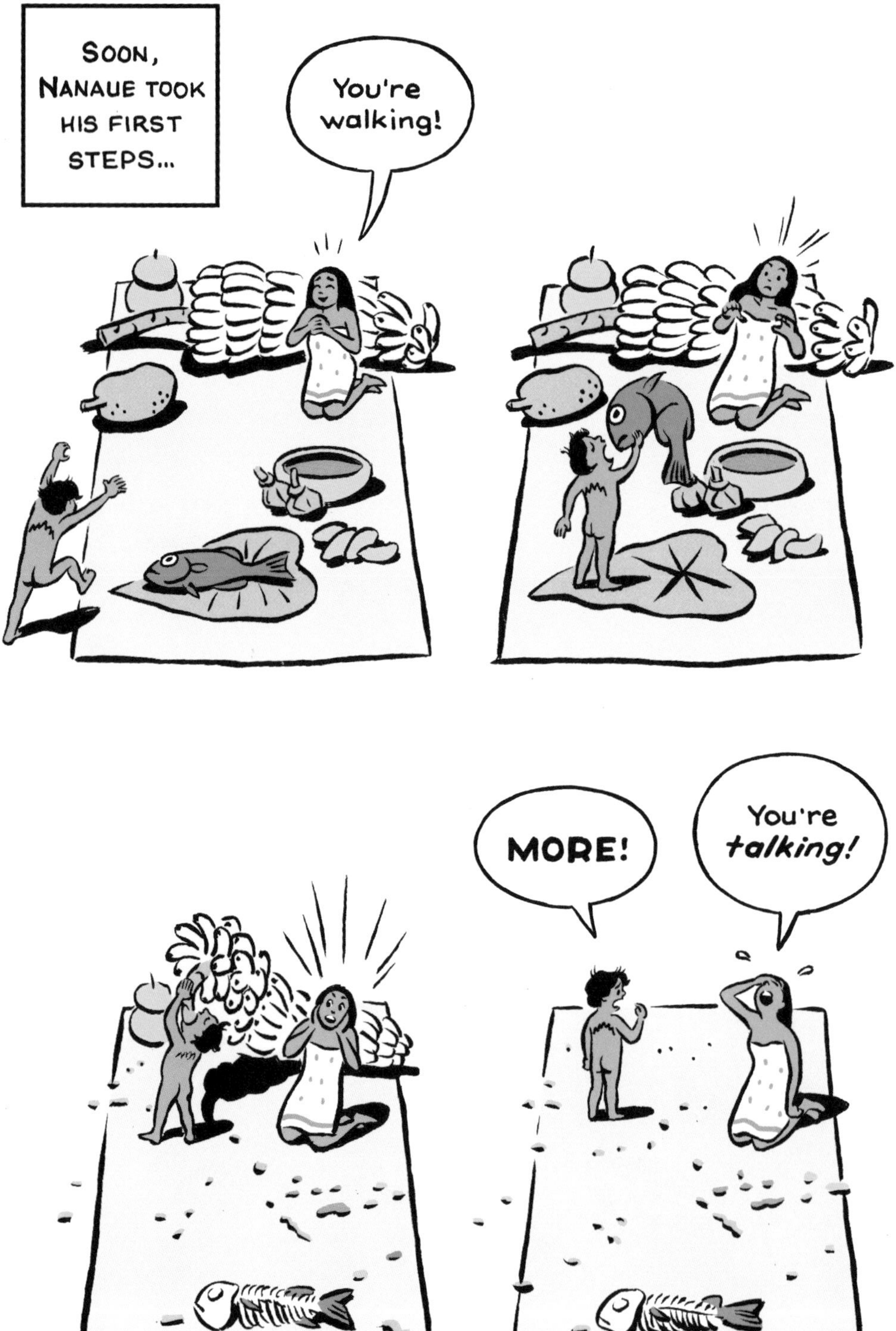
SOON, NANAUE TOOK HIS FIRST STEPS...
You're walking!
MORE!
You're *talking*!

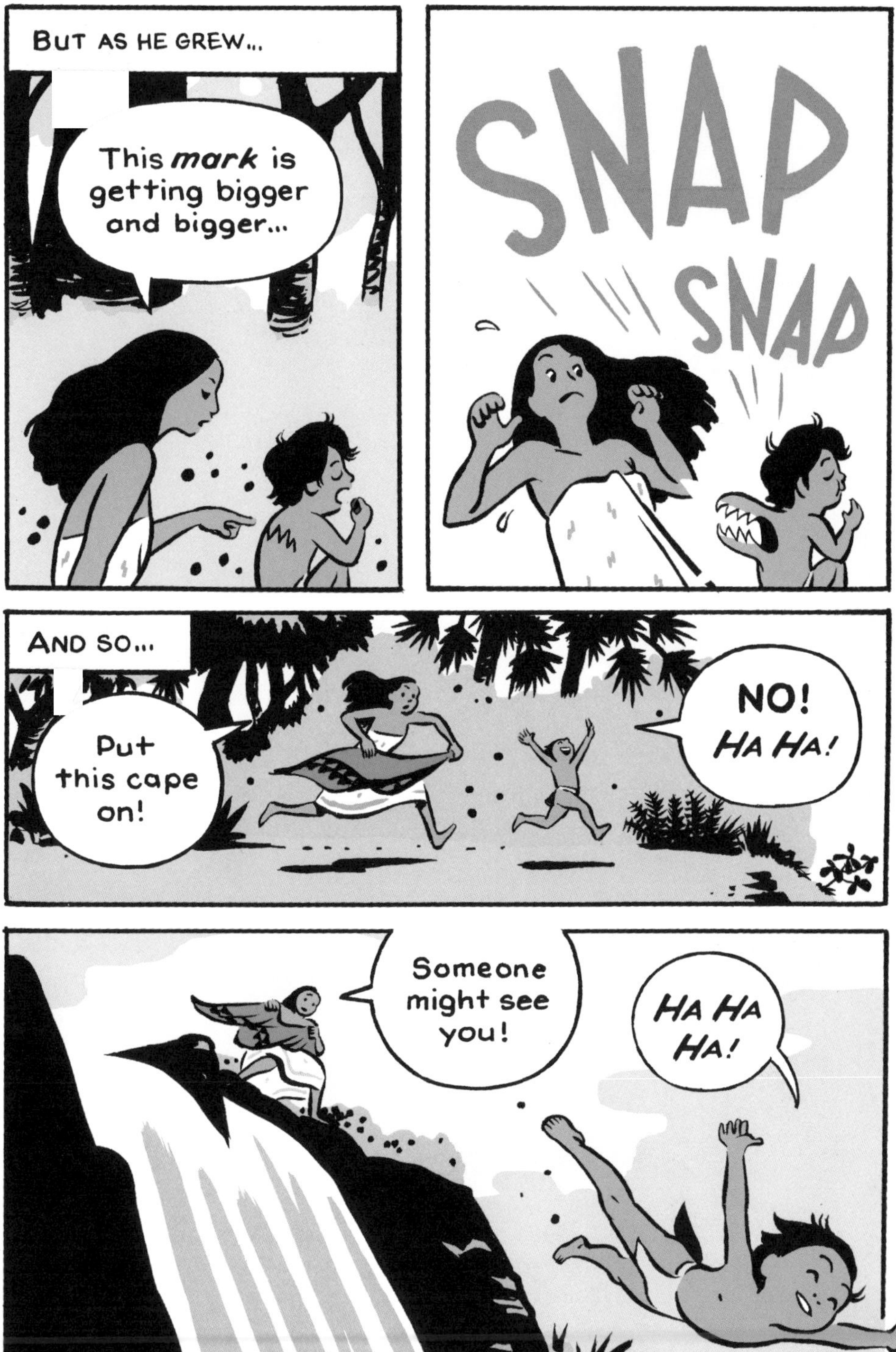

BUT AS HE GREW...
This *mark* is getting bigger and bigger...
SNAP
SNAP
AND SO...
Put this cape on!
NO! HA HA!
Someone might see you!
HA HA HA!

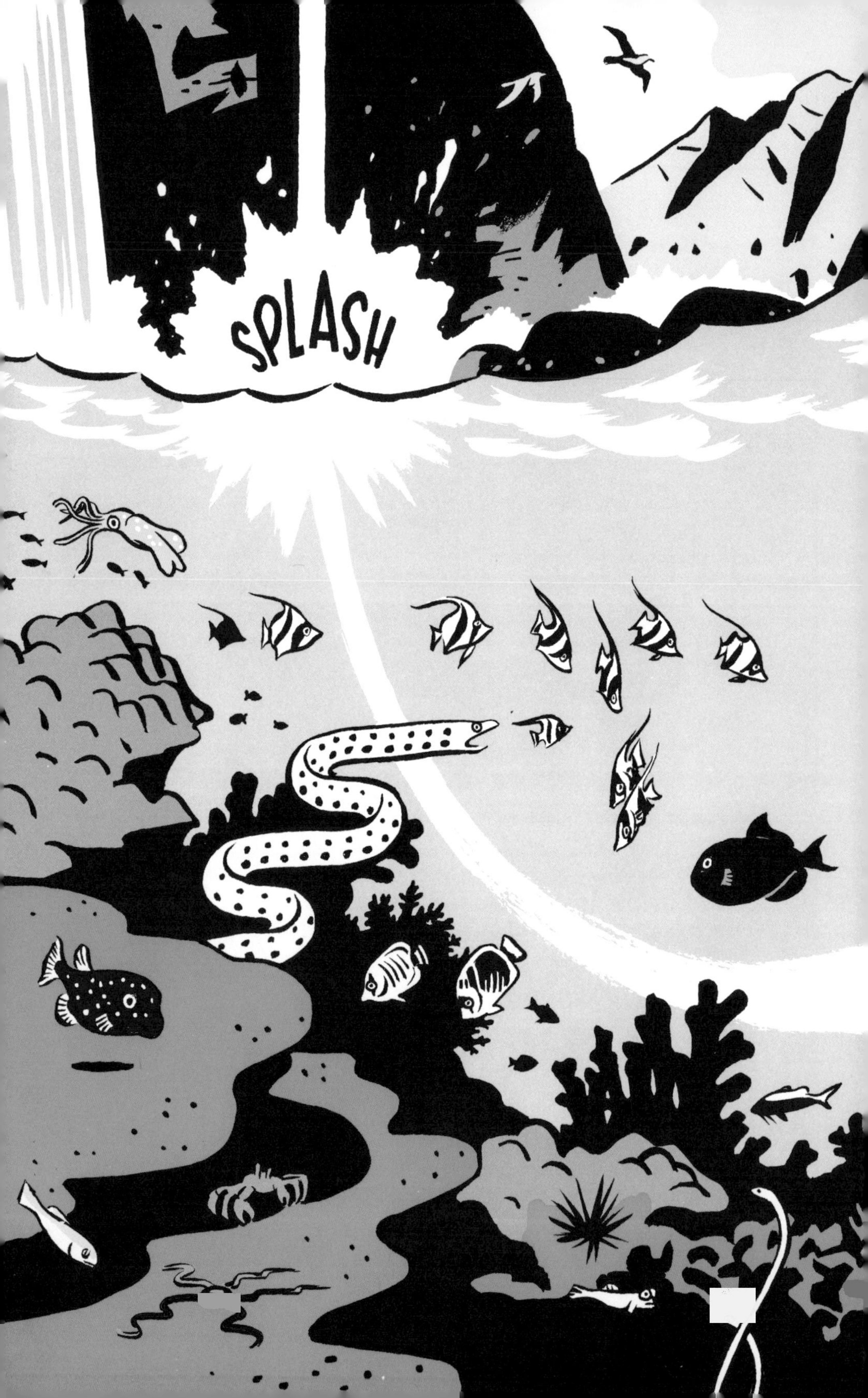
SPLASH

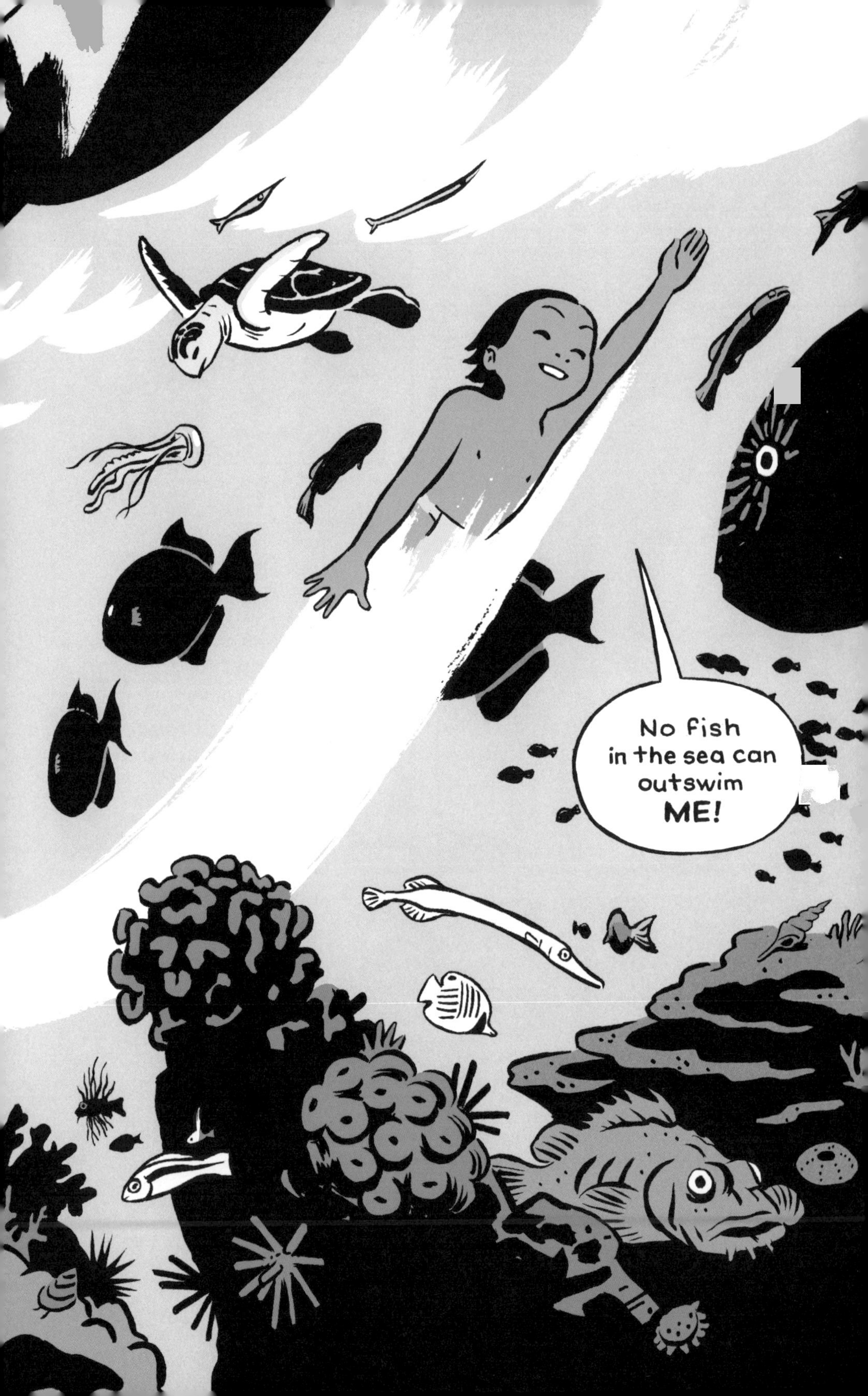
No fish in the sea can outswim ME!

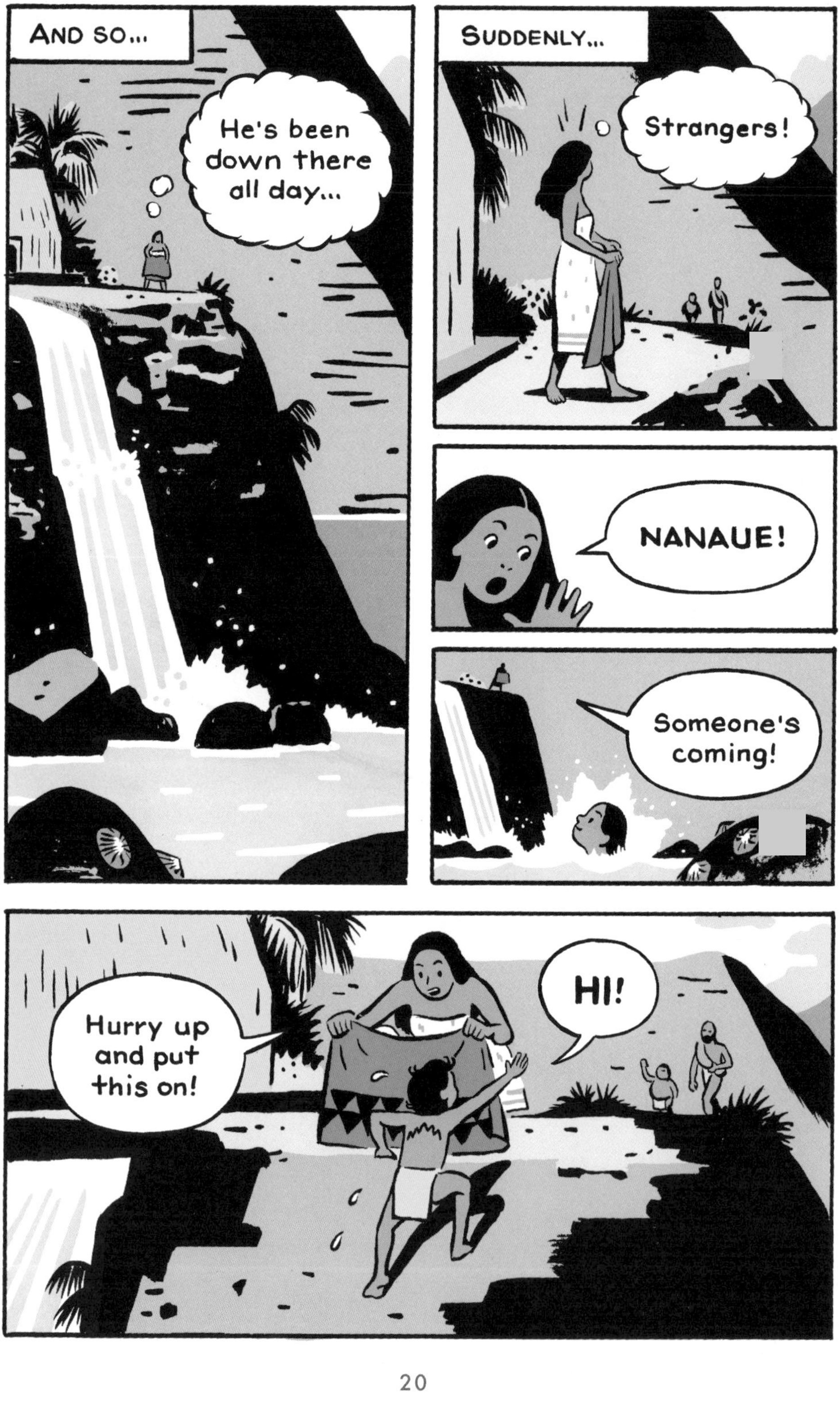
AND SO...
He's been down there all day...
SUDDENLY...
Strangers!
NANAUE!
Someone's coming!
Hurry up and put this on!
HI!

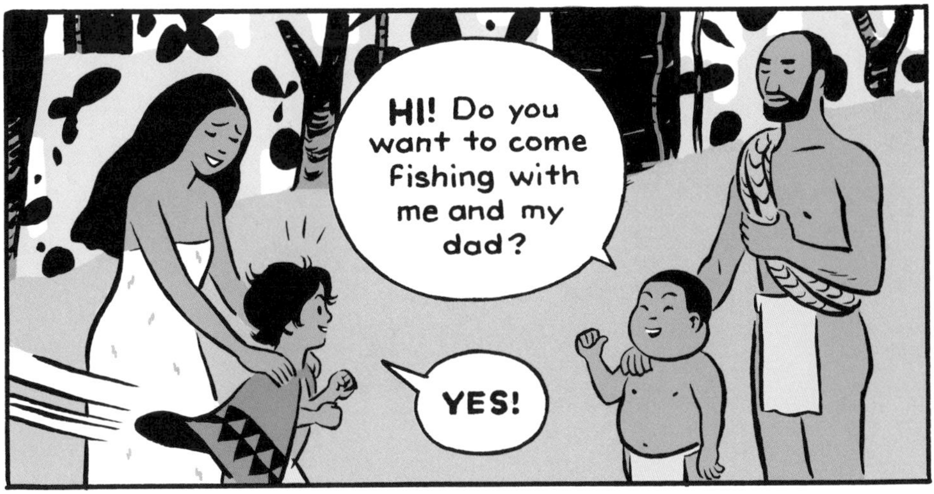
HI! Do you want to come fishing with me and my dad?
YES!

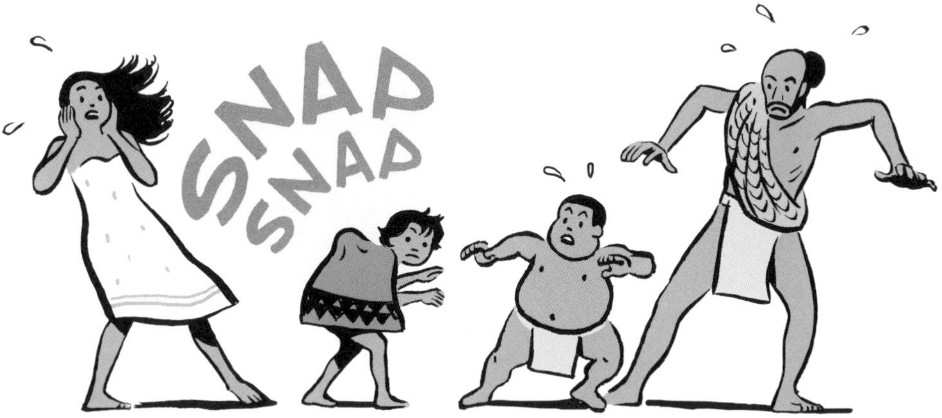
SNAP
SNAP

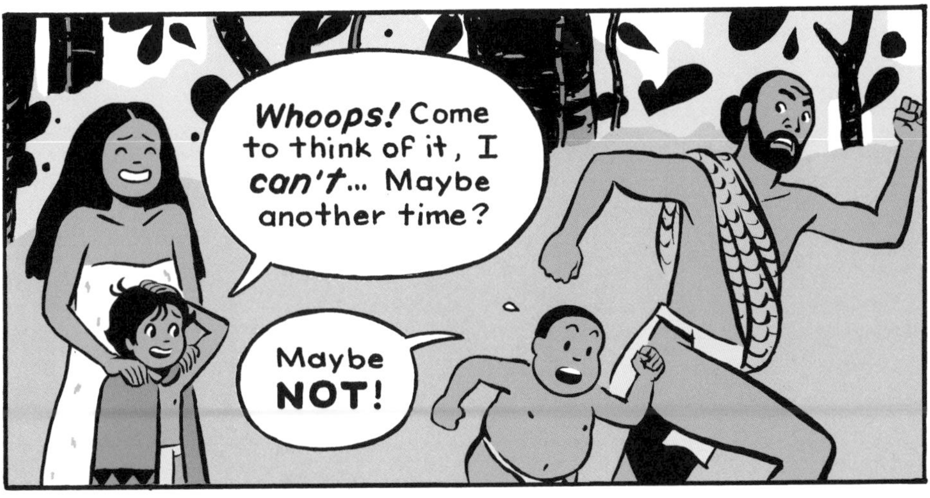
Whoops! Come to think of it, I *can't*... Maybe another time?
Maybe **NOT!**

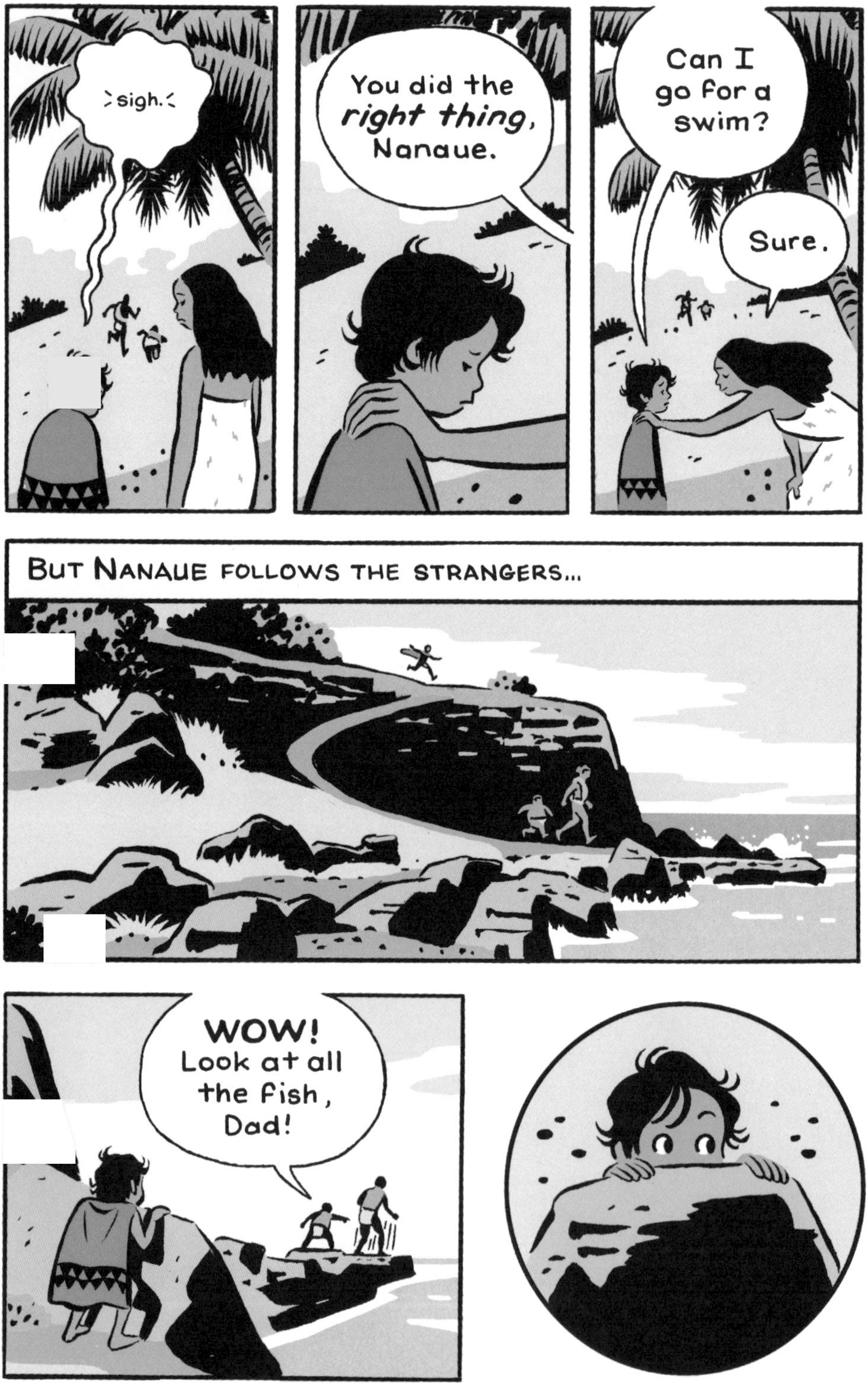
sigh.
You did the *right thing*, Nanaue.
Can I go for a swim?
Sure.
BUT NANAUE FOLLOWS THE STRANGERS...
WOW! Look at all the fish, Dad!

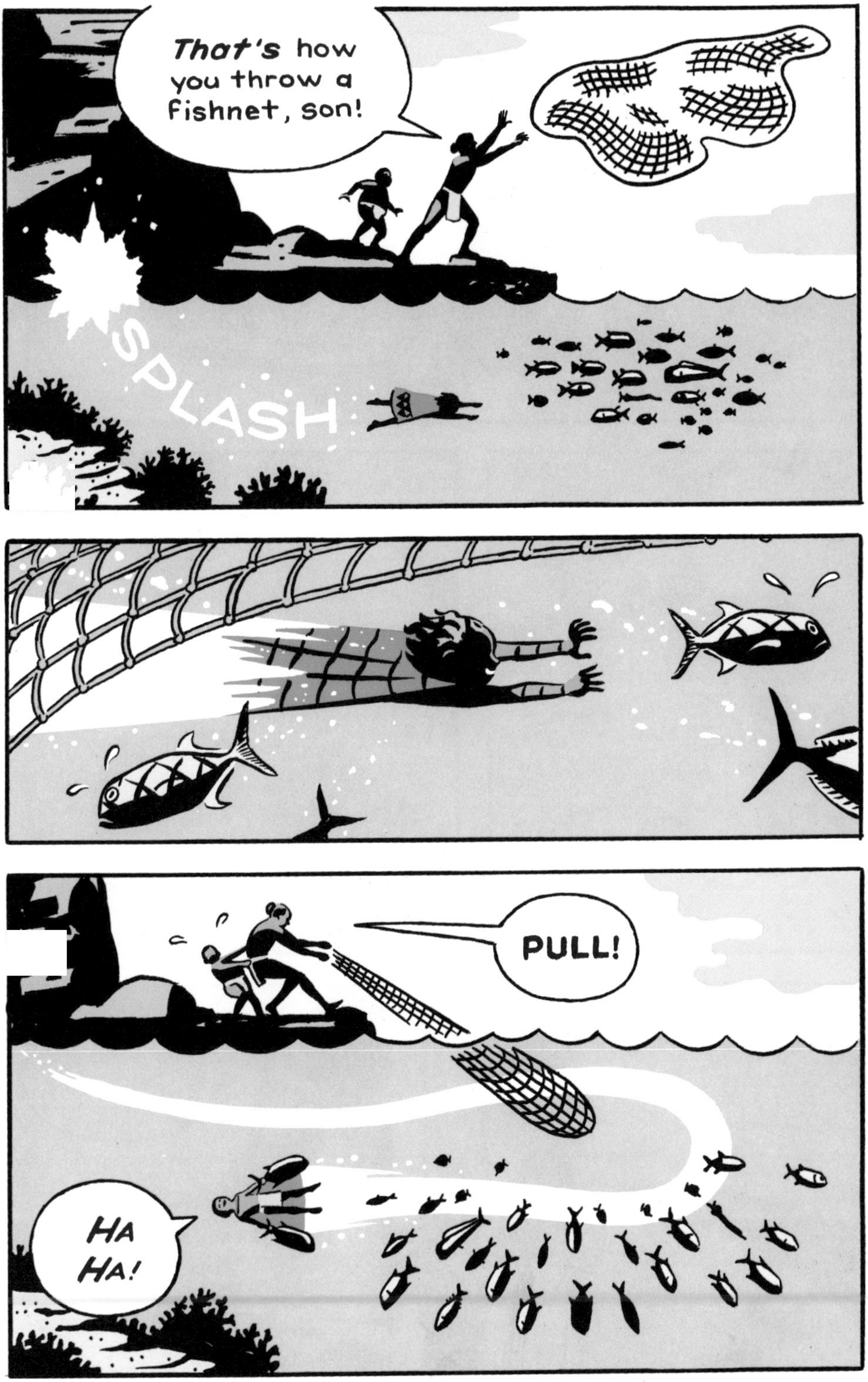
That's how you throw a fishnet, son!
SPLASH
PULL!
HA HA!

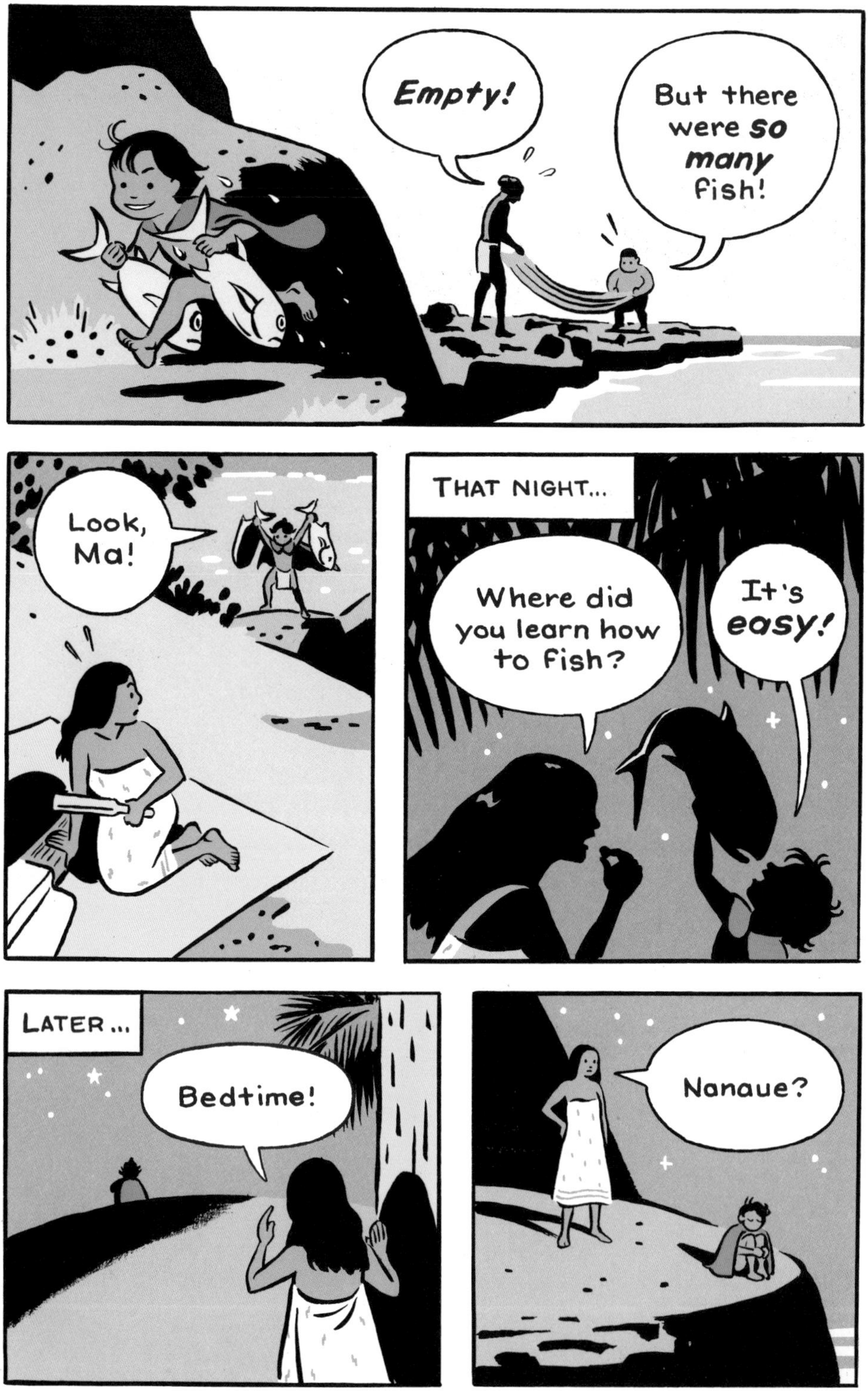

Empty!
But there were so many fish!
Look, Ma!
THAT NIGHT...
Where did you learn how to fish?
It's easy!
LATER...
Bedtime!
Nanaue?

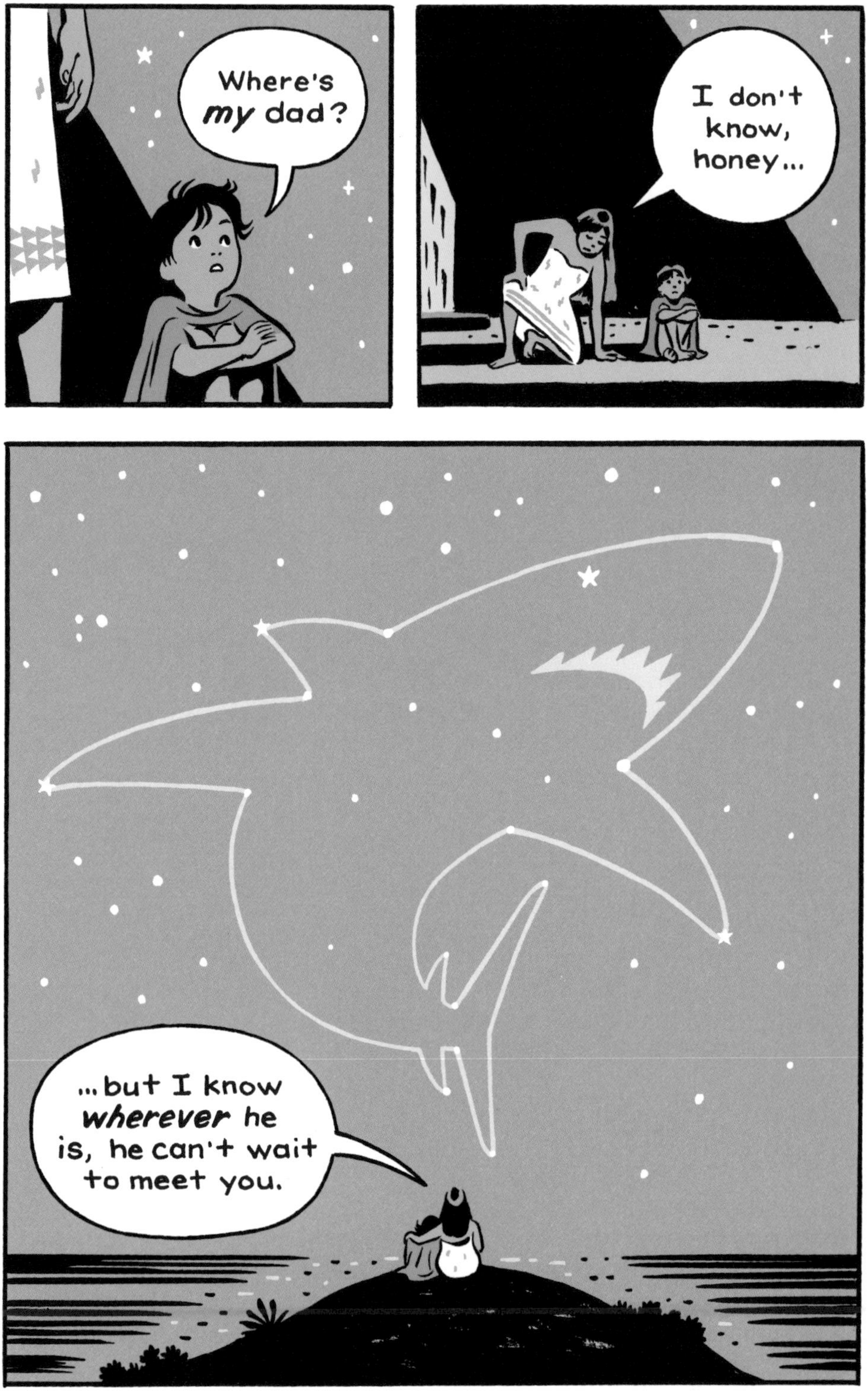
Where's *my* dad?
I don't know, honey...
...but I know *wherever* he is, he can't wait to meet you.

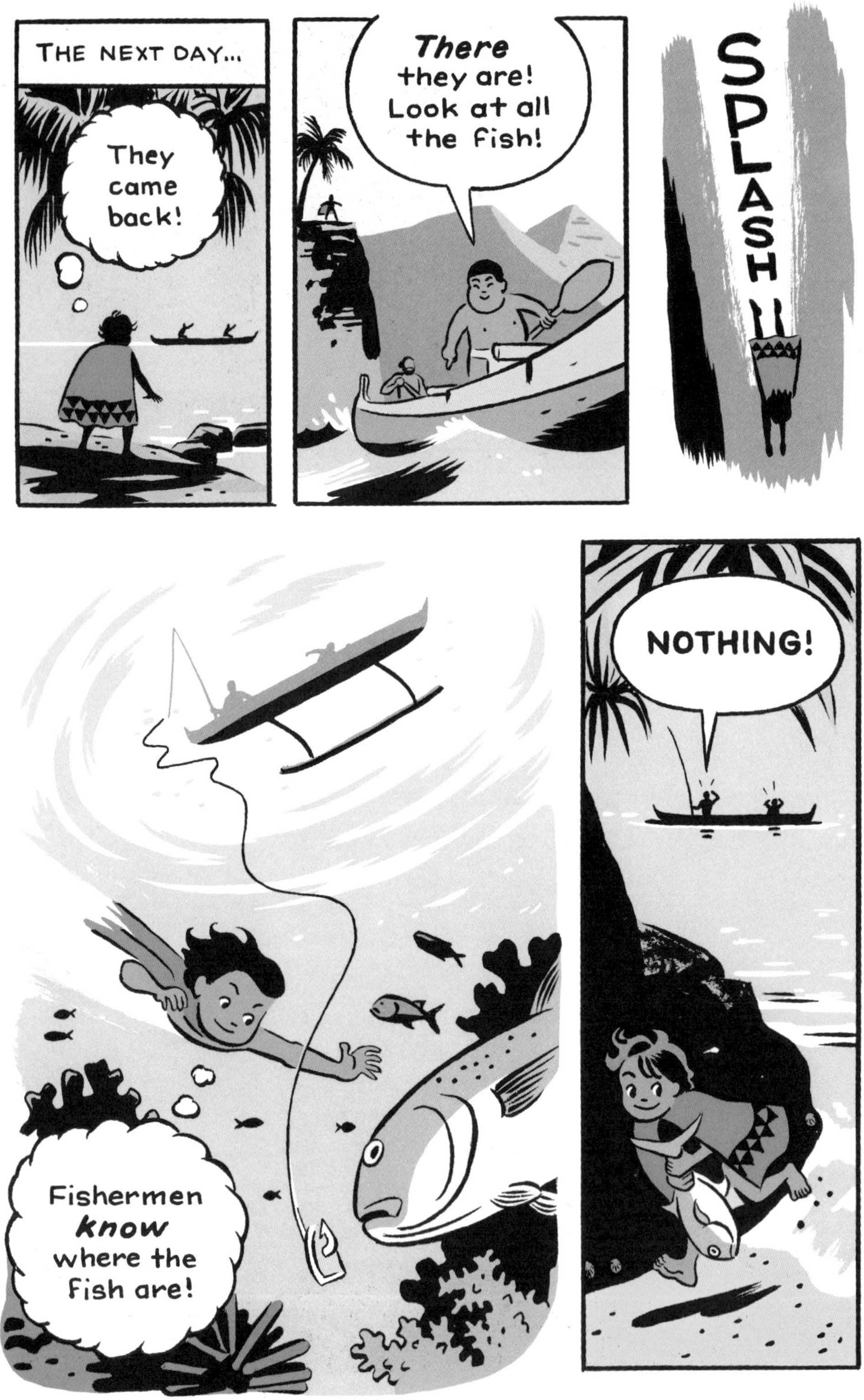
THE NEXT DAY...
They came back!
There they are! Look at all the fish!
SPLASH
Fishermen know where the fish are!
NOTHING!

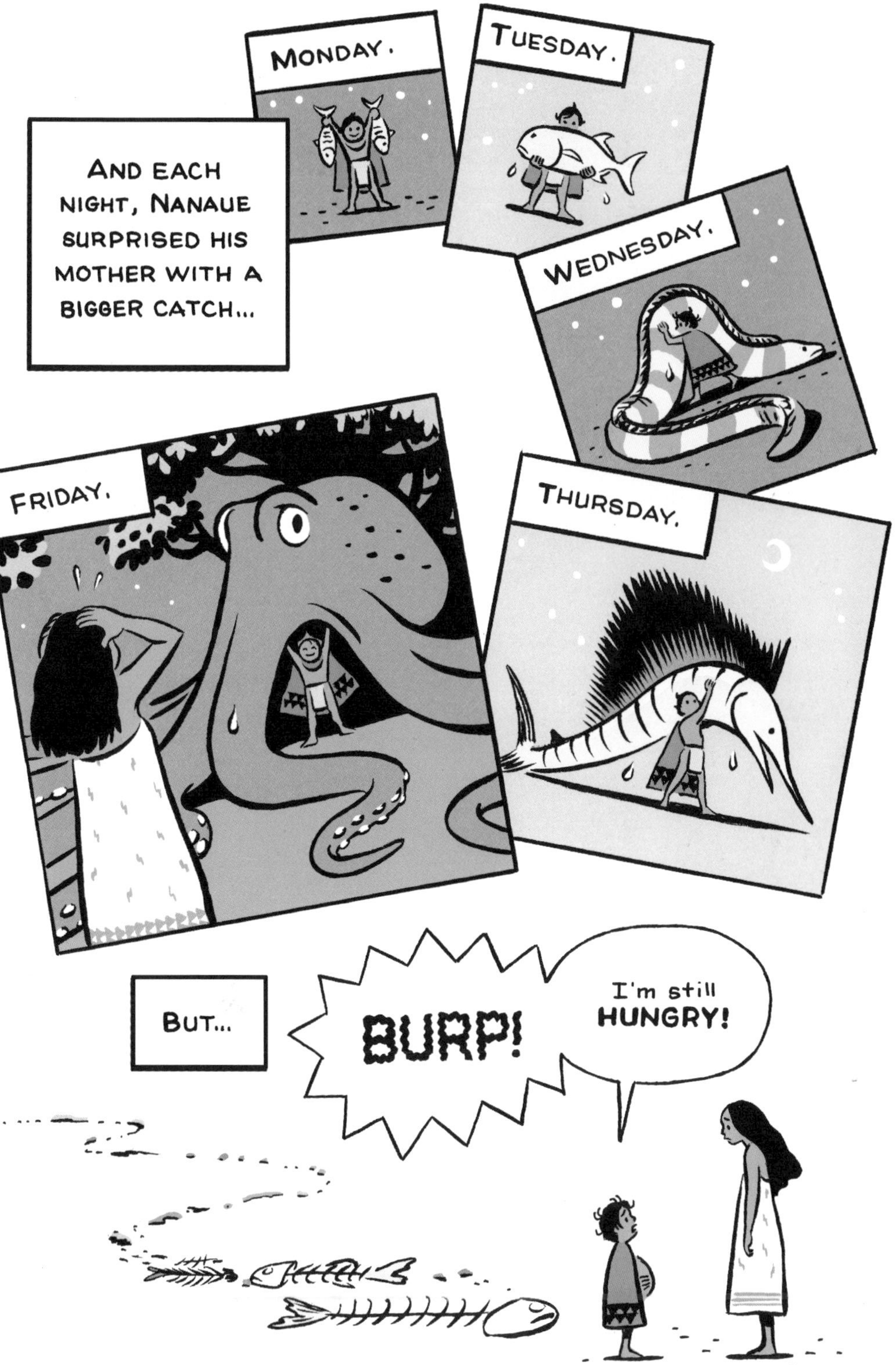

And each night, Nanaue surprised his mother with a bigger catch...
Monday.
Tuesday.
Wednesday.
Thursday.
Friday.
But...
BURP!
I'm still HUNGRY!

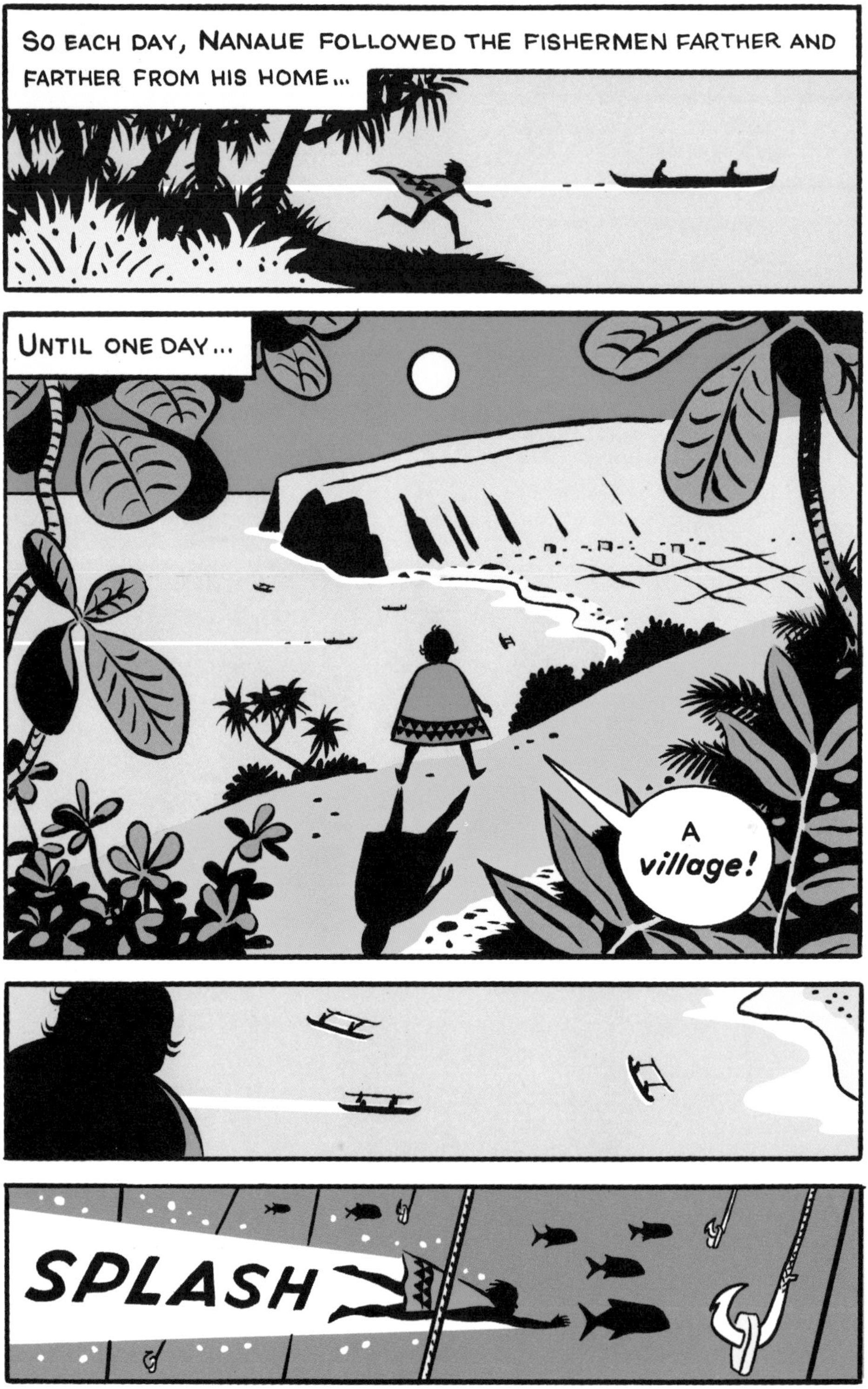

SO EACH DAY, NANAUE FOLLOWED THE FISHERMEN FARTHER AND FARTHER FROM HIS HOME...
UNTIL ONE DAY...
A village!
SPLASH

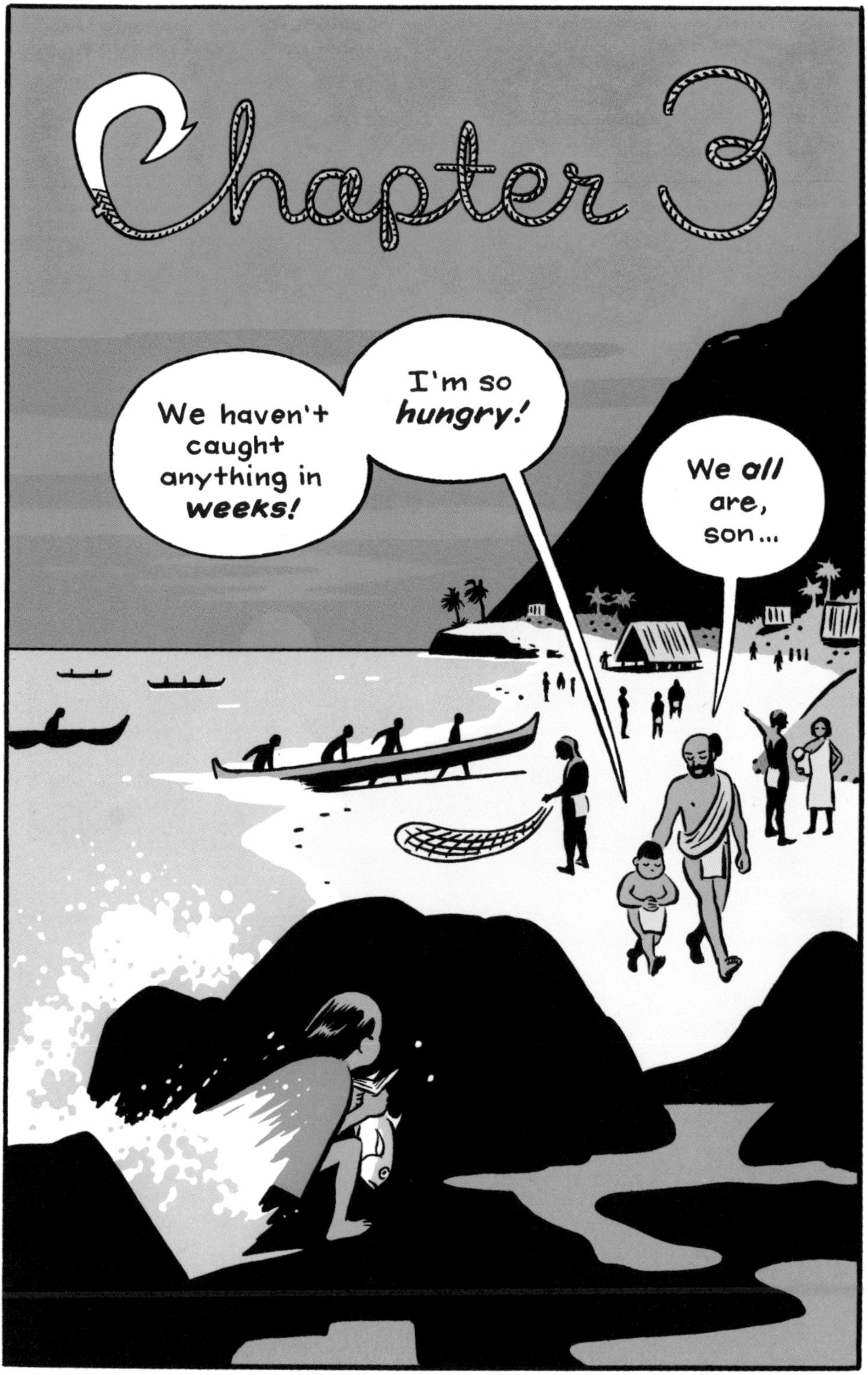
Chapter 3
We haven't caught anything in *weeks!*
I'm so *hungry!*
We *all* are, son...

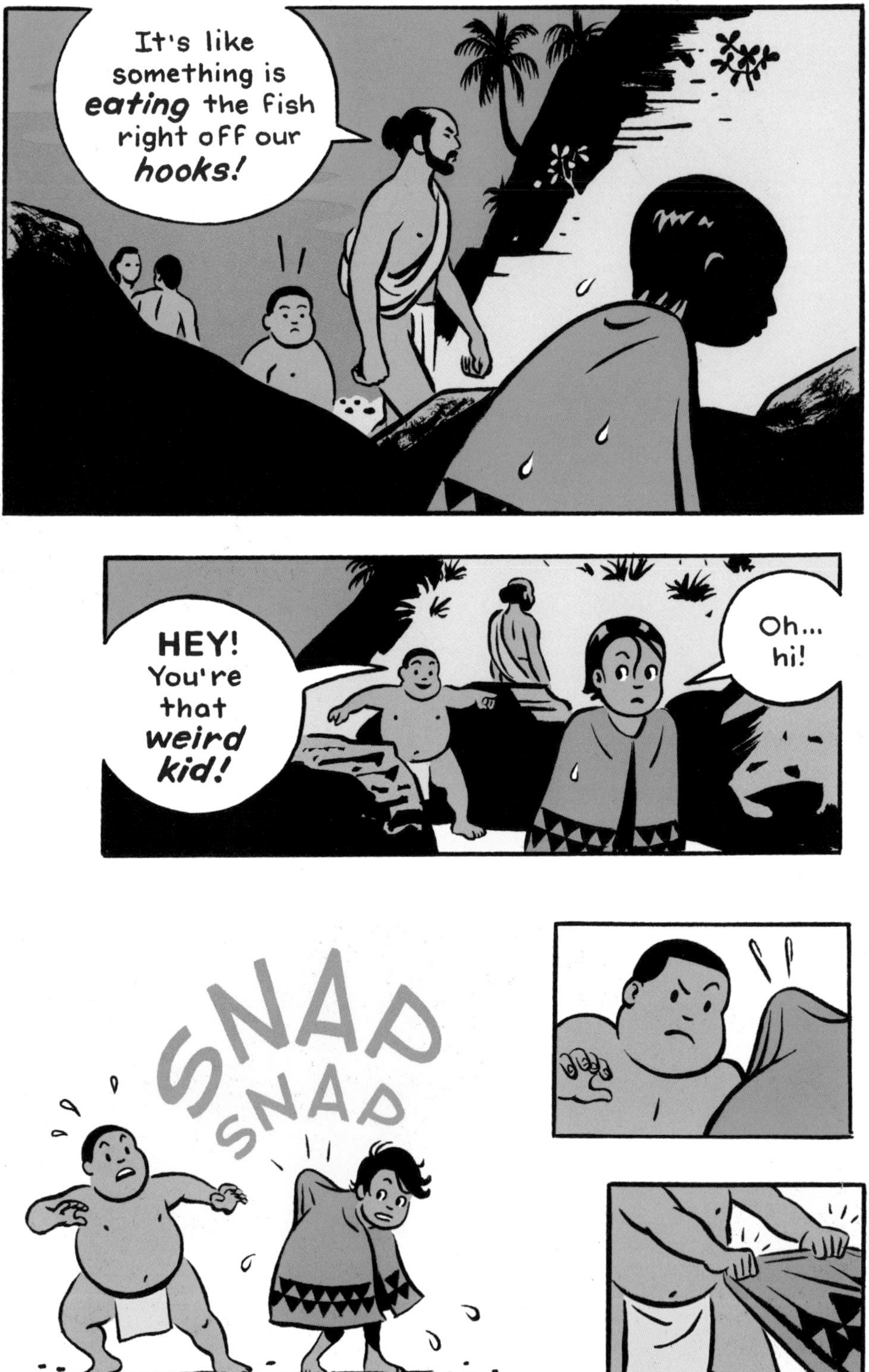
It's like something is *eating* the fish right off our *hooks!*
HEY! You're that *weird kid!*
Oh... hi!
SNAP
SNAP

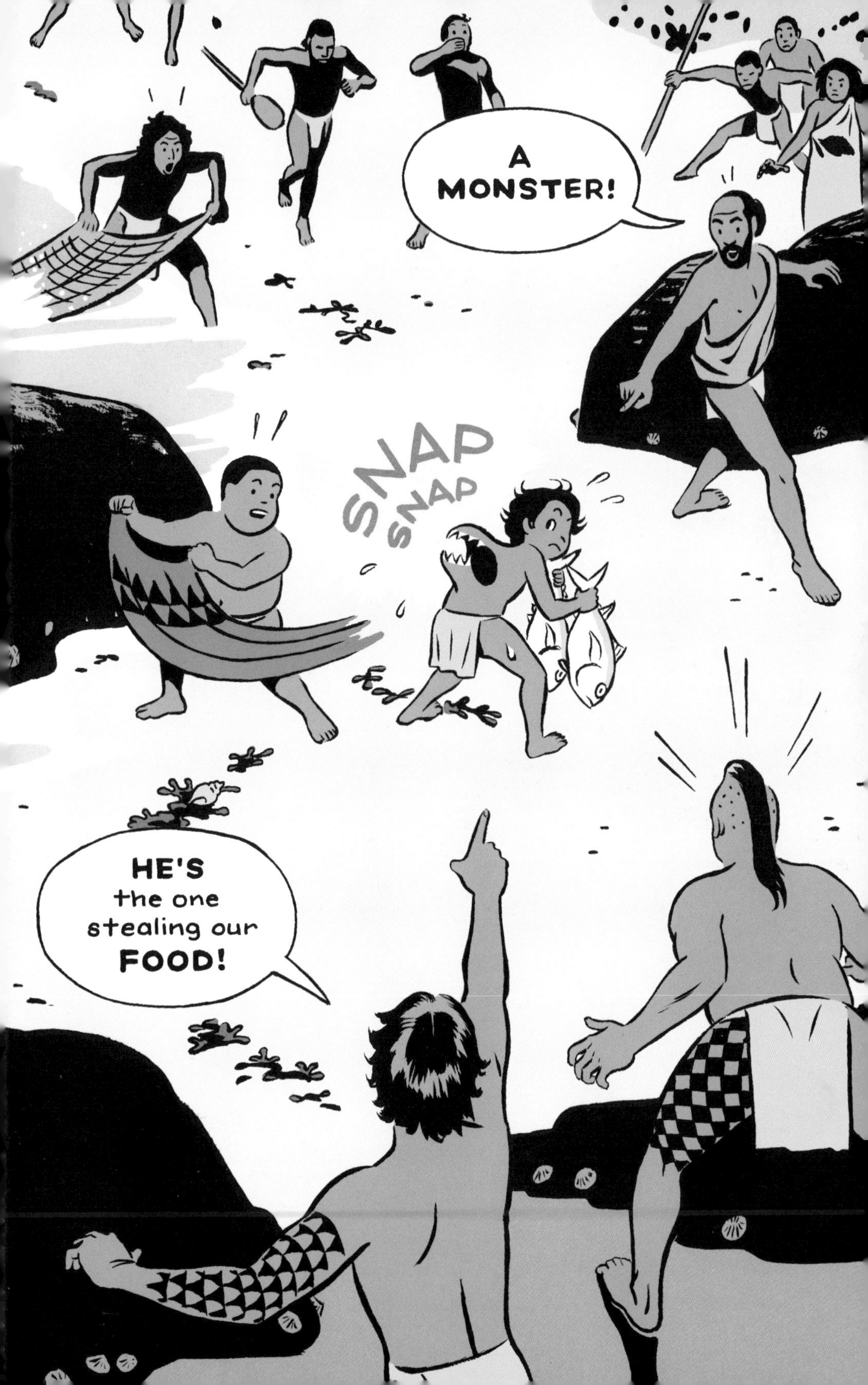
A MONSTER!
SNAP
SNAP
HE'S the one stealing our FOOD!

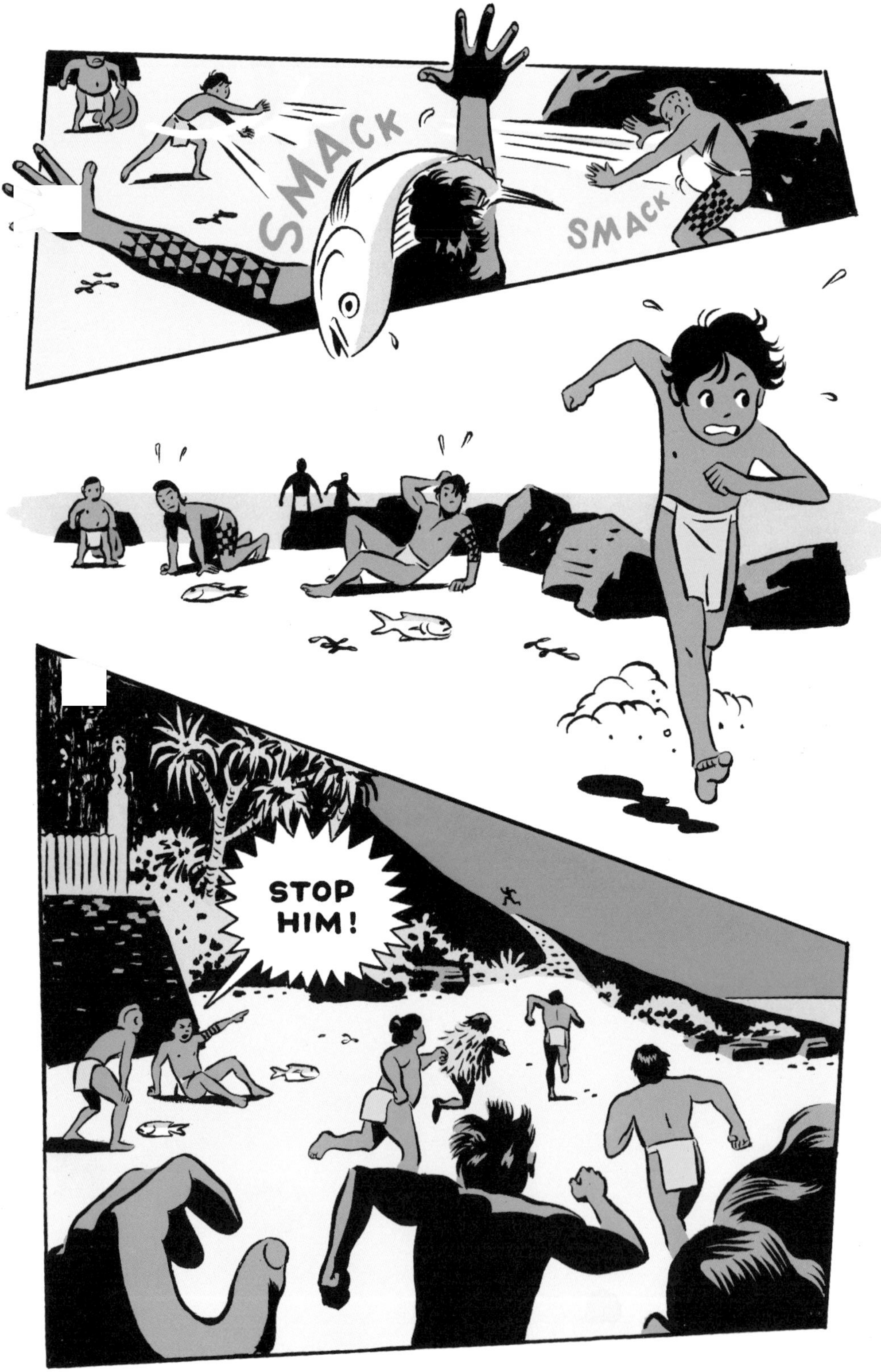
SMACK
SMACK
STOP HIM!

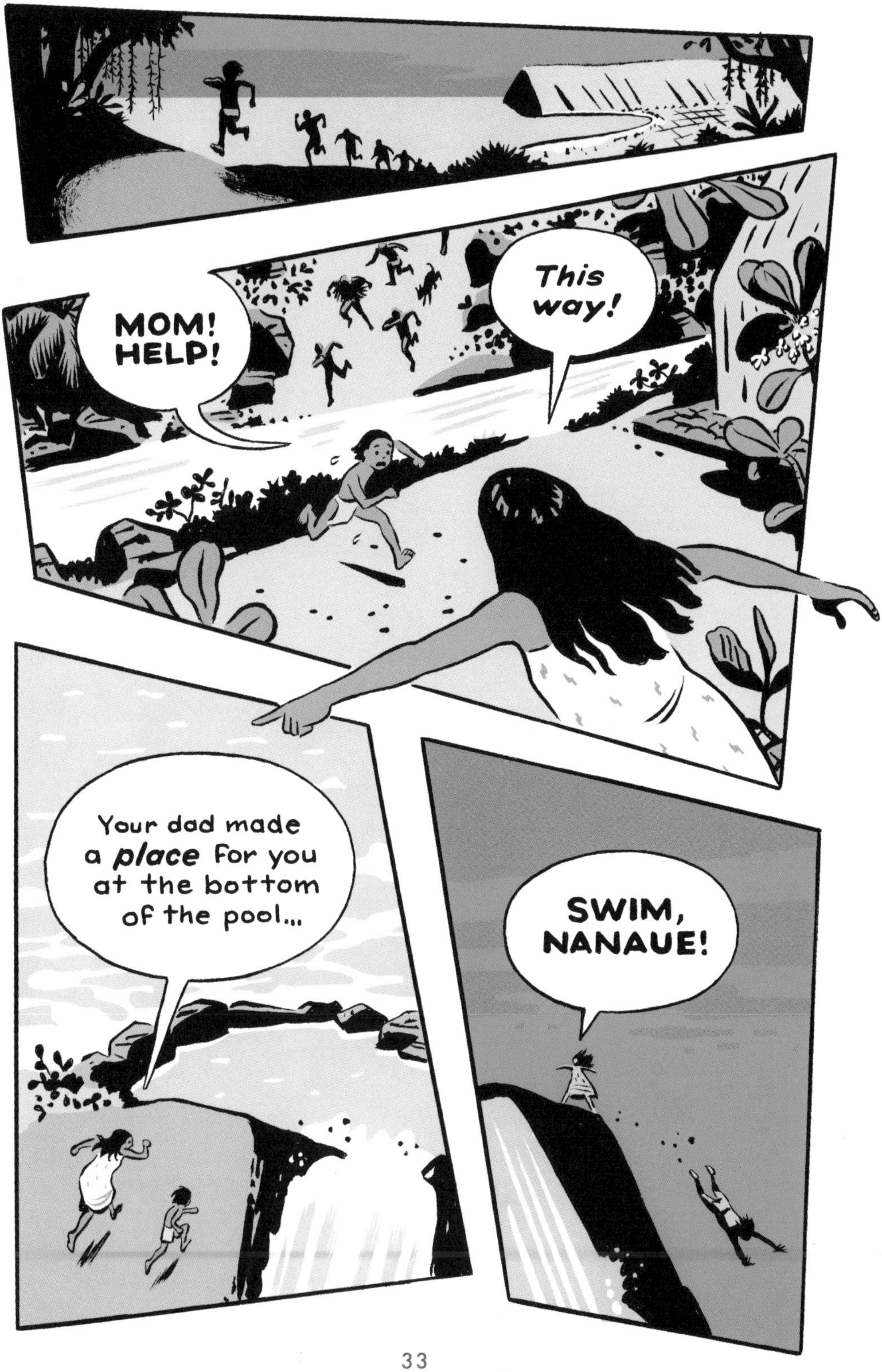
MOM! HELP!
This way!
Your dad made a *place* for you at the bottom of the pool...
SWIM, NANAUE!

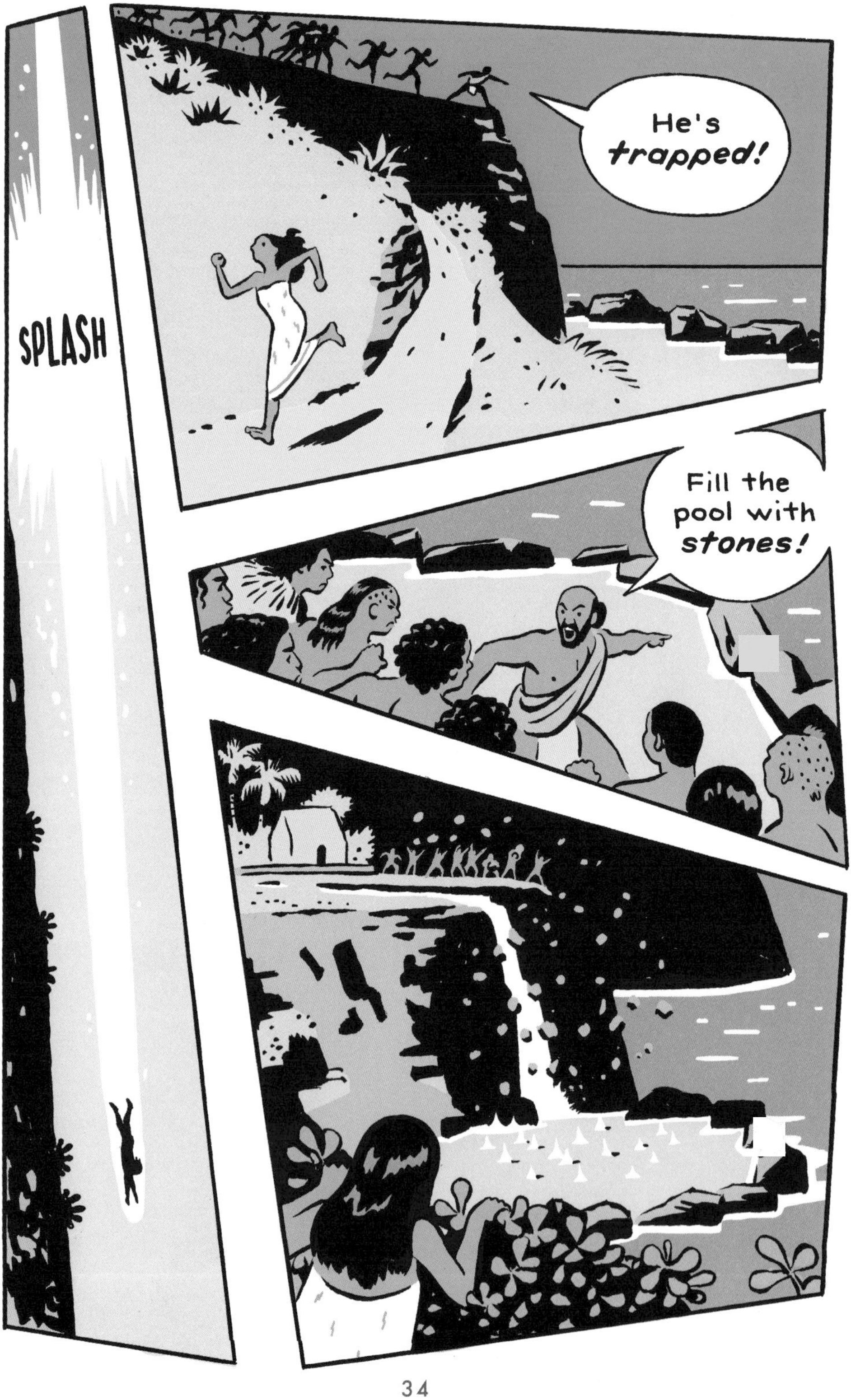
SPLASH
He's *trapped!*
Fill the pool with *stones!*

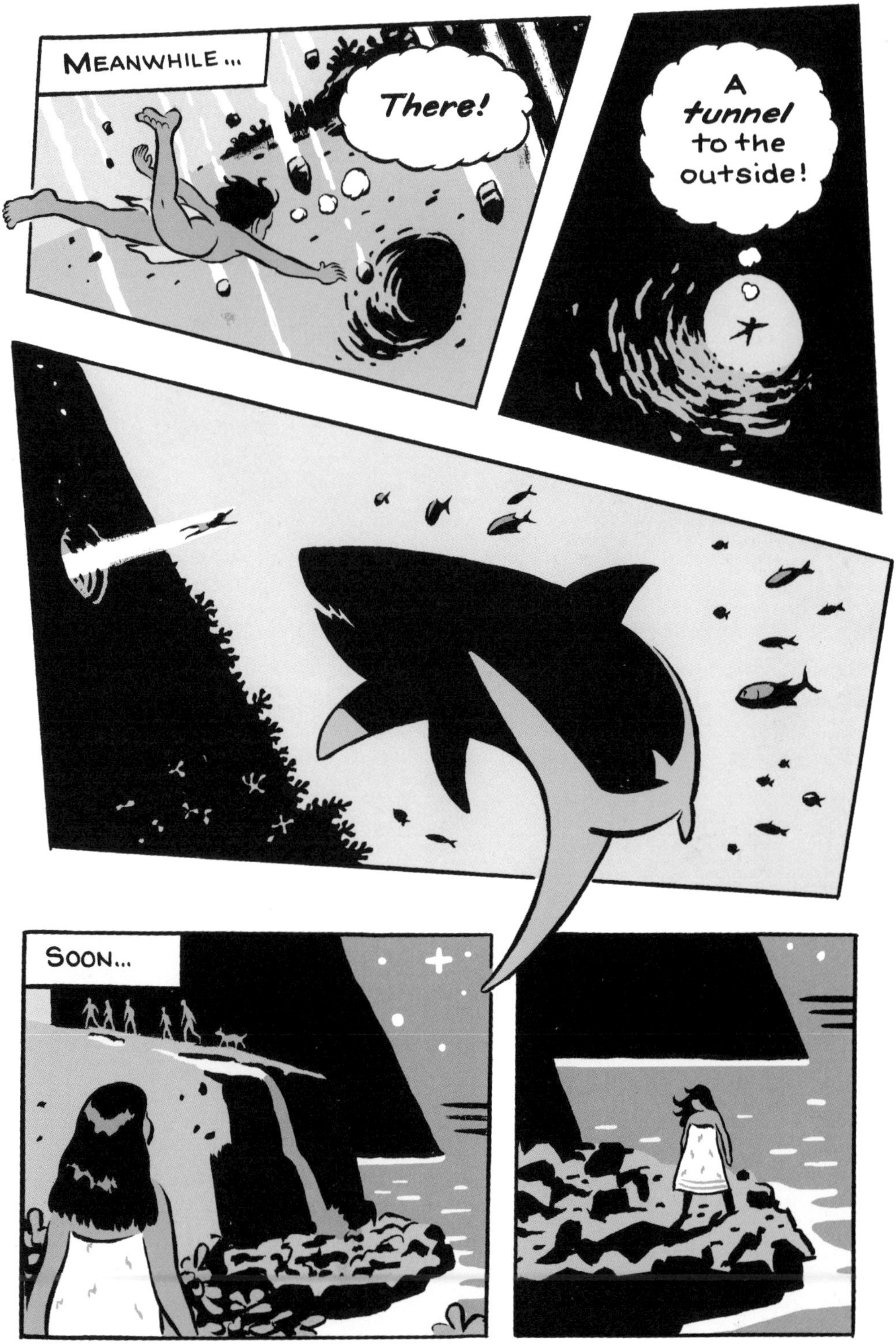
MEANWHILE...
There!
A tunnel to the outside!
SOON...

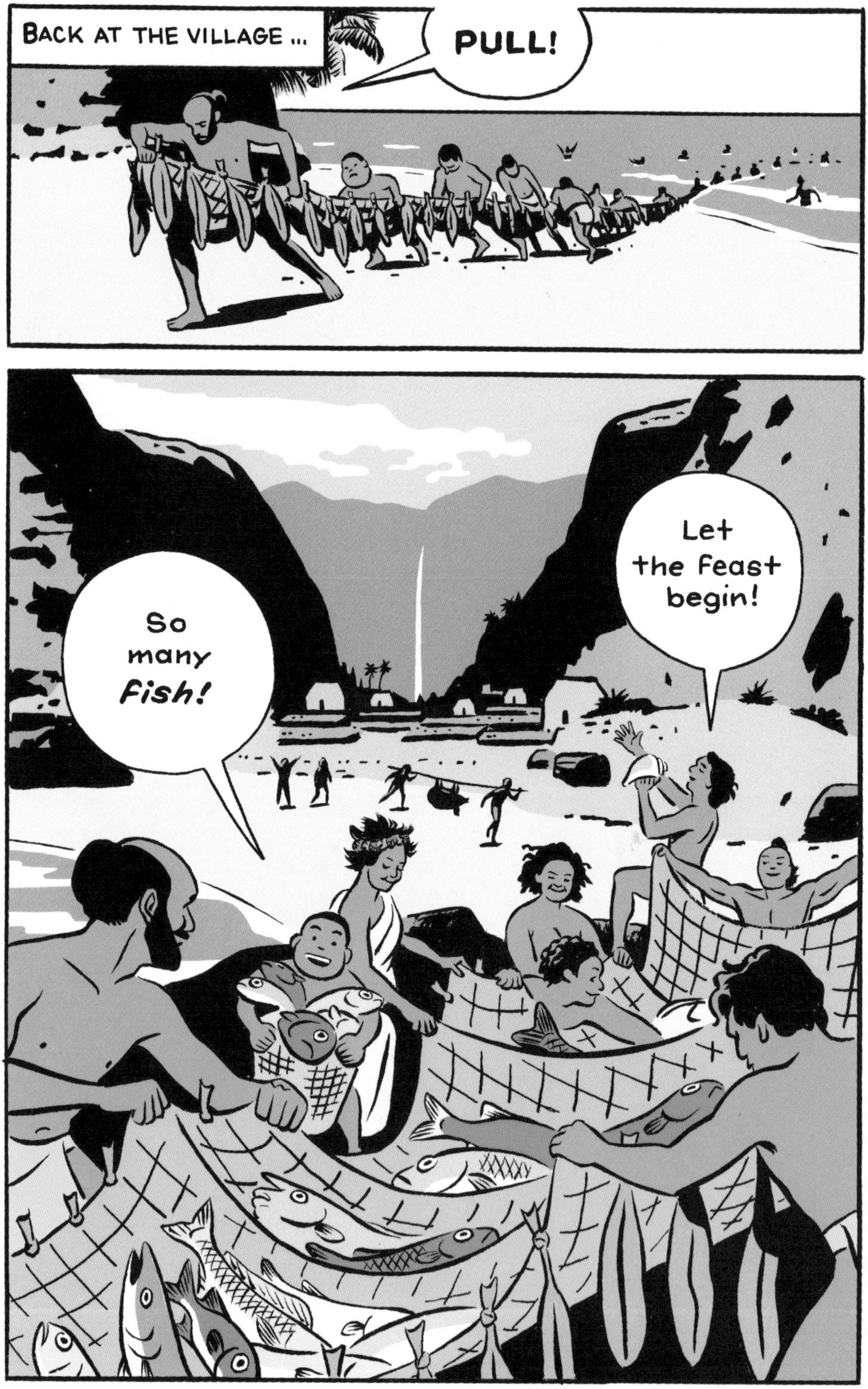
BACK AT THE VILLAGE ...
PULL!
So many *Fish!*
Let the feast begin!

TIME PASSED...

AND ONE DAY...

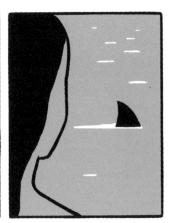

The *cape!*

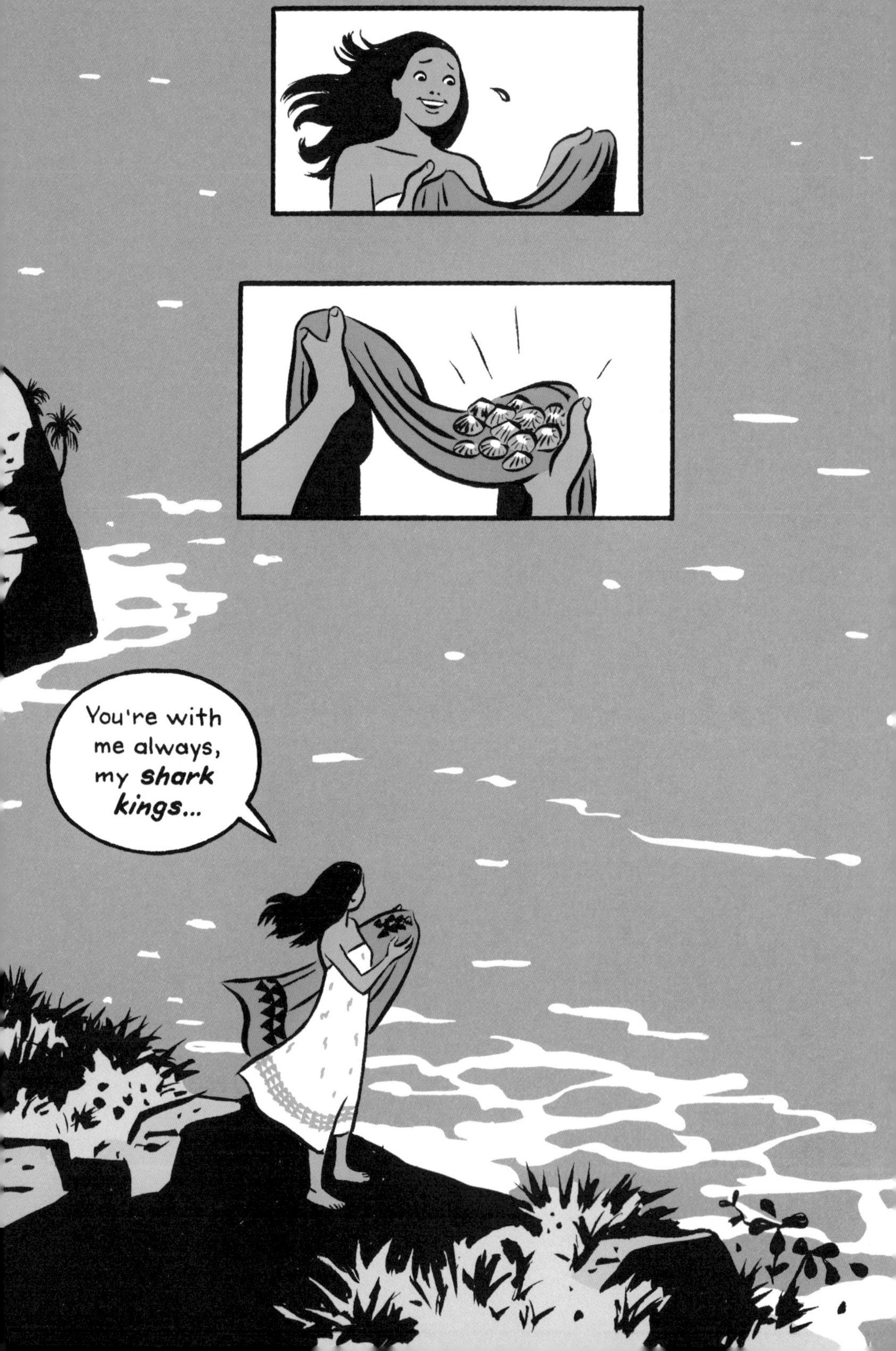
You're with me always, my *shark kings...*

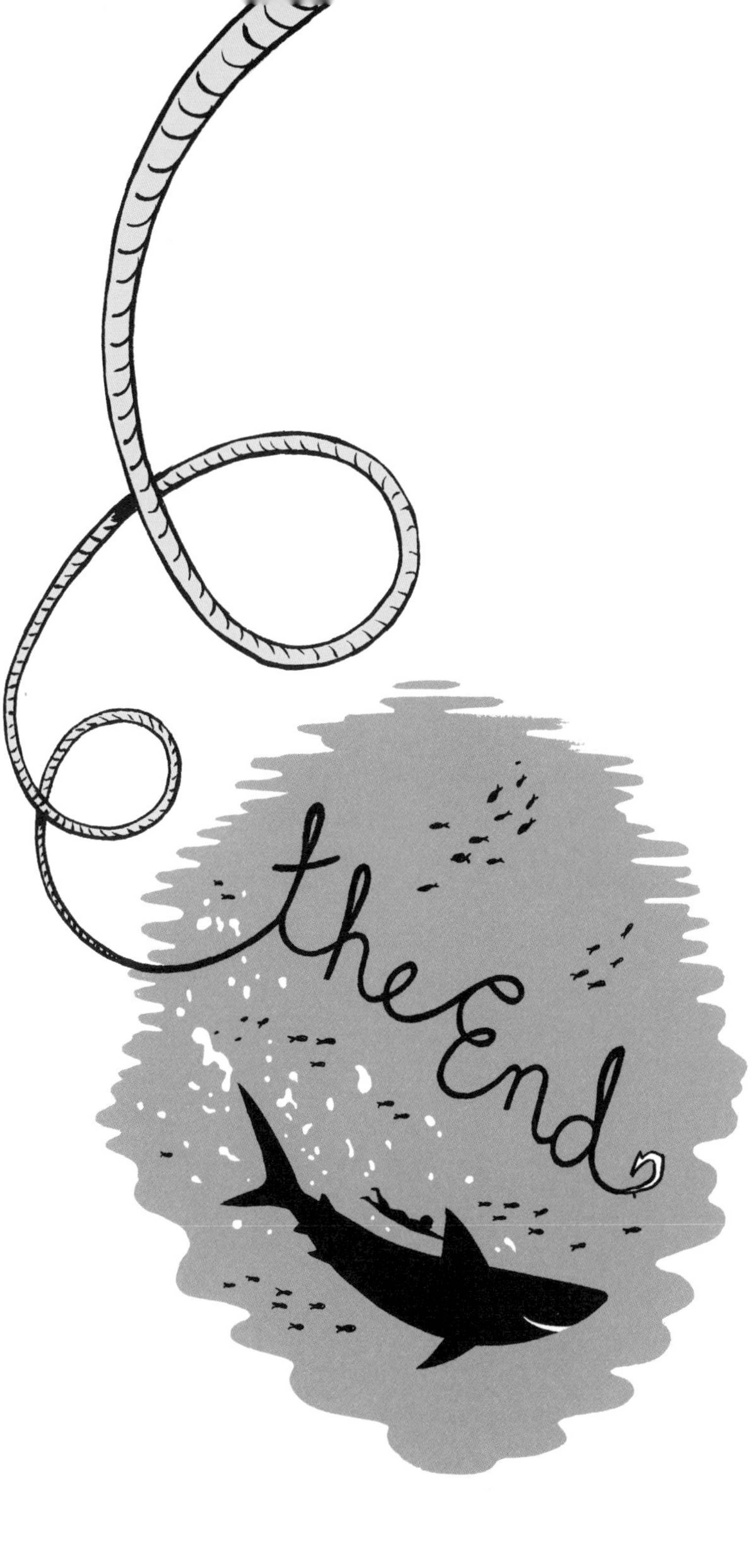
the End

ABOUT THE AUTHOR

R. KIKUO JOHNSON grew up in Hawaii on the island of Maui. For generations, native Hawaiians have told tales of the shape-shifting shark god, Kamohoalii; *The Shark King* is the artist's version of one such tale about the insatiable appetite of Kamohoalii's son, Nanaue. Kikuo's 2005 graphic novel, *Night Fisher*—also set in Hawaii—earned him both the Russ Manning Most Promising Newcomer Award and a Harvey Award. Kikuo spent his childhood exploring the rocky shore in front of his grandmother's house at low tide and diving with his older brother. Since moving to the mainland, Kikuo has discovered the joys of swimming in fresh water and currently lives in Brooklyn, New York, where he enjoys cooking, playing his ukulele, and riding his bike all over the city.

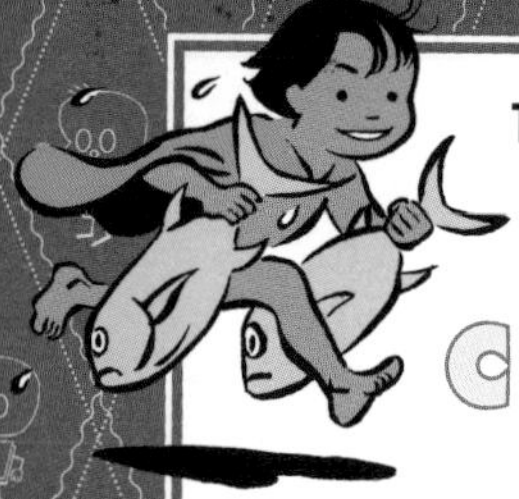

TIPS FOR PARENTS AND TEACHERS:

HOW TO READ COMICS WITH KIDS

Kids *love* comics! They are naturally drawn to the details in the pictures, which make them want to read the words. Comics beg for repeated readings and let both emerging and reluctant readers enjoy complex stories with a rich vocabulary. But since comics have their own grammar, here are a few tips for reading them with kids:

GUIDE YOUNG READERS: Use your finger to show your place in the text, but keep it at the bottom of the speaking character so it doesn't hide the very important facial expressions.

HAM IT UP! Think of the comic book story as a play and don't hesitate to read with expression and intonation. Assign parts or get kids to supply the sound effects, a great way to reinforce phonics skills.

LET THEM GUESS. Comics provide lots of context for the words, so emerging readers can make informed guesses. Like jigsaw puzzles, comics ask readers to make connections, so check a young audience's understanding by asking, "What's this character thinking?" (but don't be surprised if a kid finds some of the comics' subtle details faster than you).

TALK ABOUT THE PICTURES. Point out how the artist paces the story with pauses (silent panels) or speeded-up action (a burst of short panels). Discuss how the size and shape of the panels carry meaning.

ABOVE ALL, ENJOY! There is of course never one right way to read, so go for the shared pleasure. Once children make the story happen in their imagination, they have discovered the thrill of reading, and you won't be able to stop them. At that point, just go get them more books, and more comics.

WWW.TOON-BOOKS.COM

SEE OUR FREE ONLINE CARTOON MAKERS, LESSON PLANS, AND MUCH MORE.

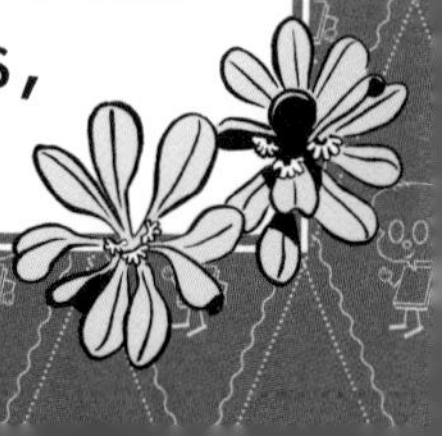